A Home Subscription! It's the easiest and most convenient way to get every one of the exciting Coventry Romance Novels! ...And you get 4 of them FREE!

You pay nothing extra for this convenience: there are no additional charges...you don't even pay for postage! Fill out and send us the handy coupon now, and we'll send you 4 exciting Coventry Romance novels absolutely FREE!

SEND NO MONEY, GET THESE
FOUR BOOKS
FREE!

C1081

MAIL THIS COUPON TODAY TO:
COVENTRY HOME
SUBSCRIPTION SERVICE
6 COMMERCIAL STREET
HICKSVILLE, NEW YORK 11801

YES, please start a Coventry Romance Home Subscription in my name, and send me FREE and without obligation to buy, my 4 Coventry Romances. If you do not hear from me after I have examined my 4 FREE books, please send me the 6 new Coventry Romances each month as soon as they come off the presses. I understand that I will be billed only $9.00 for all 6 books. There are no shipping and handling nor any other hidden charges. There is no minimum number of monthly purchases that I have to make. In fact, I can cancel my subscription at any time. The first 4 FREE books are mine to keep as a gift, even if I do not buy any additional books.

For added convenience, your monthly subscription may be charged automatically to your credit card.

☐ Master Charge **42101**　　　　　　　　　　　　　☐ Visa **42101**

Credit Card # _____

Expiration Date _____

Name _____
　　　　　　　　　　　　　(Please Print)

Address _____

City _____ State _____ Zip _____

Signature _____

☐ Bill Me Direct Each Month **40105**

Publisher reserves the right to substitute alternate FREE books. Sales tax collected where required by law. Offer valid for new members only.
Allow 3-4 weeks for delivery. Prices subject to change without notice.

The Queen's Quadrille

GEORGINA GREY

FAWCETT COVENTRY • NEW YORK

THE QUEEN'S QUADRILLE

Published by Fawcett Coventry Books, a unit of CBS
Publications, the Consumer Publishing Division of CBS Inc.

Copyright © 1981 by Georgina Grey

ISBN: 0-449-50212-0

Printed in the United States of America

First Fawcett Coventry printing: October 1981

10   9   8   7   6   5   4   3   2   1

The
Queen's Quadrille

Chapter 1

"I declare, my dear," Lady Didright announced emphatically, "sometimes I think that you and I are the only members of this family with a shred of common sense!"

"But, Mama, surely it is only natural that Elizabeth should have her head turned a bit by all this excitement," Amelia said dryly. "After all, it is her coming-out."

"Your sister has approached her first Season as though it were a four-month bacchanalia," Lady Didright replied sharply. "It is all very well to be fond of balls and parties, but she has developed an unhealthy passion for them. And as for your brother . . ."

"Randolph must sow a few wild oats," Amelia observed.

"As for that, my dear, you are only quoting your

grandfather and you know what *he* is! All this talk about the pranks he was up to fifty years ago does no one any good. Wild oats, indeed! I remember dear Mama telling me that he was a perfect scandal until she married him and put him right. Why, anyone would think he was still a young man about town instead of teetering on the thin edge of seventy."

Amelia could present no argument to that. Ever since he had been widowed five years before and come to live with them in the country, her grandfather had developed a penchant for reminiscence and, when they had removed to London for the purpose of presenting Elizabeth to Society, he had begun to think of little else beside his riotous youth, regaling anyone who would listen with stories made all the more outrageous for having the unmistakable touch of truth about them.

Indeed, as she watched her mother pace about the sitting room of the house which they had rented on Portman Square, Amelia was predisposed to sympathize. It had been no easy matter for the older woman to take on the burden of bringing up three children when she had been widowed ten years before. And now to have had to accept the responsibility of an aging parent who was dedicated to the incessant review of a scandalous past was a burden at best, particularly since her nature was one of the utmost rectitude.

"I should not worry so," Lady Didright said suddenly, pausing beside her elder daughter, her brown eyes tied to one another with a web of wrinkles which had come from constant frowning, "if it were not for the example the young Prince sets. In the ordinary way of things, I would be glad enough that Randolph is regarded as his friend. But the young men who make up the Prince's circle are not respectable. There, I *will* say it, even though Elizabeth claims I am old-fashioned."

Amelia considered how best she could distract her mother from a recital of the latest scandals surrounding the young heir to the throne. She was a tall, slim girl with jet black curls showing beneath her mobcap. Although she had not inherited her mother's dour features, it was Amelia's misfortune to be regarded more often as sensible than pretty by her mother who was convinced that ladies could not conceivably be both. Elizabeth, for example, had been doomed to be called giddy from the moment she had emerged into girlhood complete with golden hair and angelic features, and Randolph was handsome enough to cause his mother constant worry. But, disregarding her elder daughter's classic oval face and thickly-fringed blue eyes, Lady Didright's greatest compliment was that Amelia was sometimes pretty enough, but not so often as to interfere with common sense.

"You must be my support in these trying times, my dear!" was her constant cry and, although Amelia often grew weary of it, she kept her own counsel, knowing the thin line between her mother's pothering and outright hysteria. The year before, when she herself had been presented, her mother had taken her to London for only a single week to see to the formalities of her coming out and nothing more.

"I cannot bear to see your head turned, my dear," had been her excuse. "Why, I depend on you so much! Besides, you would not care for the world of the *haut ton*. You are too sensible . . ."

Sometimes Amelia thought that she would scream if she heard that word again. Granted that much which she had seen in London had struck her as absurd. Fops and dandies and ladies of fashion made a great deal too much of their narrow world and took themselves too seriously by far. Tempests in teapots became world-shaking events. But on the whole, she thought, it did little harm and often Society was amusing.

But to her mother's puritanical eye there was danger lurking everywhere. And when Amelia demanded why, given her opinion of London Society, her mother had not kept the family in the depth of Sussex at Random Hall, the ancestral seat, she was met with the response that Elizabeth and Randolph must marry.

"You know there is no one suitable for either of them in the country," Lady Didright would wail. "Would you have your brother make a match with the vicar's daughter and Elizabeth take up with the local doctor? The truth is that one of the prime purposes of a London Season is to bring eligible young people together and I can only hope that in the process neither Randolph nor your sister will be corrupted. Of course, I know I can depend on you since you are so very sensible."

It had entered Amelia's head from time to time

of late that she would like to do something so completely outrageous that her mother could no longer label her in such a convenient fashion. This thought was always followed promptly, however, by the lurking suspicion that she did, indeed, have too much common sense to do anything of the sort.

"The Prince," her mother was saying now, "leads a very fast life indeed. I will not speak of particulars but I do not care for Randolph associating with Lord Barrymore and his brothers. As for the sister, I would not care to tell you the stories I have heard! And yet the Prince makes them his favorite friends."

There was no need, Amelia thought, for her mother to speak of details. All London buzzed of the behavior of Lord Barrymore who had been nicknamed "Hellgate" because of certain eccentricities which included having four magnificently dressed Africans play the French horn during his hunting chase, shifting the signs of public houses to confuse the customers, and racing his chaise-and-four at a terrific pace to the danger of every pedestrian in sight. One brother was called "Cripplegate," being lame, and another brother went as "Newgate," that being, reportedly, the only prison in the country at which he had not been accommodated. As for the sister, the Prince himself called her by the *sobriquet* "Billingsgate" since, despite her high estate, she had as ready a supply of oaths as anyone who lived in that particular London slum.

"Your grandfather calls the Barrymores fun-loving rascals," Lady Didright continued. "How can I convince Randolph that he must take a more sober view? For instance, he intends to be in the Prince's company at Vauxhall tonight. And Elizabeth will have it that she intends to go with him. You must help me, Amelia. Indeed, you must!"

Lady Didright was a little woman with many of the nervous mannerisms of an English sparrow. She paced and darted and was never still until she was literally forced into a corner. Her gowns were chosen with an eye to making her inconspicuous, and she favored gray. Although tall turbans were the fashion among matrons of her age, hers were so flat as to be little more than slight protrusions on her small head, and her face was constantly caught in an expression of extreme anxiety. Amelia could not recall a time when she had not been torn between a sense of irritation and a feeling that she should somehow protect this little woman who took life so seriously.

"Mama," she said now in an attempt at reassurance. "Vauxhall is a respectable enough pleasure garden and you know that there are fireworks and music and all manner of entertainment of the sort that can do no one any harm."

"La, my dear!" Lady Didright exclaimed, taking three steps forward and two to the side for no better purpose except to move. "I have heard that gentlemens' pockets may well be picked there and that a lady must hold quite tightly to her reticule."

"Surely the same circumstances exist on a crowded afternoon on Bond Street, Mama," Amelia said patiently.

"And then there are the ladies of the evening," Lady Didright continued, taking little hops toward the window. "Oh dear! Oh dear! The more I think of it, the more perturbed I am!"

It was not the first time that Amelia had seen her mother whip herself up in this very manner and she knew the consequences if she were not reassured.

"There are jades everywhere, Mama," she declared. "Besides, Elizabeth told me that there are to be a number of the Prince's friends in attendance and that they will keep themselves apart. Why, the very presence of the Prince will distinguish them. And the Duchess of Devonshire will be one of the party. An older woman."

Lady Didright knotted up her face in a manner which made it clear that the presence of the Duchess of Devonshire offered her no particular reassurance.

"Very well, Mama," Amelia said. "If you are determined to be concerned, either forbid Randolph and Elizabeth to go or make yourself their attendant."

And with that she started toward the door, a slim, demure figure in white muslin who gave little outward sign of her irritation. Nothing about London suited her mother. The day began and ended with complaints. And yet she would not leave the city until the Season ended. Even then, if Elizabeth and Randolph had not made matches with someone, they might not return to Random Hall. Bath was another fashionable hunting ground even though, in Lady Didright's opinion, Society there was even more dissolute than it was in London.

"Randolph assures me that if he is not agreeable, the Prince will drop him," Lady Didright wailed, skipping across the floor to place herself between her elder daughter and the door. "And Elizabeth threatened to let herself out of a window if I said she could not go! Oh, dear, they are both so headstrong! Not at all like you, my dear. That is why I have to ask a favor."

"Yes, Mama," Amelia said in a tight voice, clenching her hands behind her back. "What favor have you to ask me?"

"Why, just that you should go with them, my dear," Lady Didright said, standing on tiptoe in order to pat Amelia affectionately on one cheek. "You could make certain that everyone behaves discreetly."

Amelia stared at her mother with disbelief in her eyes. "You want *me* to be a chaperone?" she demanded.

"I only wish that you were older," Lady Didright went on, oblivious to the outrage of her elder daughter. "Still, you will turn twenty soon, and that will have to do."

With that she turned and left the room as though it had not occurred to her that Amelia might have more to say. As a consequence, minutes later, when Lord Wellingham came into the room, Amelia was in a state of outright rebellion.

"I have never disobeyed Mama in anything,"

she declared without prelude as the old man hobbled in to join her. "Indeed, you have often criticized me for being too obliging, Grandpapa! But this time I have been pushed too far!"

Lord Wellingham expressed approval with a broad smile which disclosed a handsome set of ivory teeth. Once a broad-shouldered, handsome man, he had shrunk with the years and shriveled like an aging nut until his skin was a network of fine lines. His legs, encased in old-fashioned pantaloons, were thin and bent so wide into a bow that he required a cane to walk and his bald head was covered with a periwig. But, despite the hunched shoulders and various other infirmities, he had a jaunty air about him, as though he were still the young rake who had roamed London years ago.

"Damme, it does my heart good to see you fly up into the boughs at last, my dear!" he said, lowering himself onto a chair stiffly. "I was on my way to join Queensberry, but I'll be a gudgeon if he can't wait a bit."

Another of the thorns in Lady Didright's side was the fact that not only had London refreshed her father's memories of a riotous past, but had allowed him to meet some few remaining companions of his youth. The Duke of Queensberry, or old Q as he was familiarly called, lived in palatial style in a mansion facing Green Park where, every day, he could be seen sitting in a bow window with a friend or two, surveying the passing throng on Piccadilly, openly ogling the ladies and with a groom mounted just below to ride after any acquaintance the duke might recognize and wish to exchange a word with. In his youth, Queensberry had been well known for his originality and had once arranged the construction of a carriage so light that, drawn by four blood horses, he had raced it at the unheard-of speed of nineteen miles an hour. He had had a passion for opera singers in his prime and had been remarkably generous in his patronage. But now he concentrated on conserving his strength so that, as he told Amelia's grandfather, he could spin his life out for as long as possible.

"Now, what's the trouble, child?" Lord Wellingham demanded. "You know you'll get nothing but sympathy from me. Your mother is a fine woman, 'pon my soul she is. But she will fret and worry so she drives me out of patience with her. She was the same way as a girl, you know. Always anticipating the worst. 'You are a prig, Miss,' I'd often tell her. 'You need to be more tolerant. Not everyone can be as perfect as yourself.' But she would never listen to me. Damme if she's ever listened to anyone beside herself."

Amelia was so accustomed to this familiar litany that she scarcely heard the words. Indeed, on previous occasions, her loyalty to her mother had prevented her from giving her grandfather encouragement to make any complaint. But today she was prepared to throw her customary discretion to the winds.

"I will *not* be Elizabeth's chaperone at Vauxhall," she said.

"Ah, Vauxhall!" her grandfather exclaimed. "I remember one night in '45 when young Wilks and I . . ."

"In the first place I was not even invited. I never am. Elizabeth spreads it about that I find all sorts of entertainment frivolous and Mama will tell everyone she meets that I am sensible."

"Hanger was there, as well," her grandfather went on. And Hall Stevenson, although if that was the case it must have been '44 because . . ."

"The thing is that it is so difficult to break a pattern," Amelia said. "If people *will* think of me as a model of common sense, I do not see what I can do about it. My reputation is made."

"Yes, it was '44," her grandfather declared. "But there. I've forgotten now what I was about to say. What's this you say about reputation, gel?"

"I should like to have a new one!" Amelia exclaimed, faced flushed, eyes snapping. "I do not want to be thought dependable and steady and all the rest."

"Well, if that is the only problem, my dear, you're not to worry," the old man said. "I know my mind wanders and all the rest but I am not a lobcock yet. I'll think of something. Yes! Yes! Old Q will help. What you need is to be put up to some nonsense or other. And Vauxhall is a fine place for that. If you'll take my advice, my gel, you'll appear to make a point of accepting your mama's suggestion. Leave me to come up with a plan. I'll be dashed if the very notion of it doesn't make my blood run faster!"

And, pulling himself to his feet with an effort, he hobbled from the drawing room, leaving Amelia to consider just how fortunate she really was to have her grandfather take up the cudgels in her defense with quite so much enthusiasm.

Chapter 2

Amelia considered her relationship with her sister Elizabeth as ambiguous at best. On the one hand she was fond of her younger sister and she knew her affection was reciprocated. But, no doubt because Elizabeth had so often been compared to Amelia to her disadvantage by their mother, it was only natural that there should be a certain tension between the two, particularly now when Elizabeth felt herself to be no longer just a child.

"Mama *will* call me frivolous," she often complained to Amelia. "But that is only because she has you to hold up as a contrast. You always do the right thing and so it follows that, if I do anything else, then I am wrong."

In fact it was not quite as simple as that. Elizabeth *was* frivolous. Perfectly well aware of her golden-haired beauty, she thought of nothing but new gowns and pleasure and preferred to follow impulse rather than judgment. For years Amelia had been her mentor, guiding and advising whenever difficulties arose between mother and daughter as they often did. But once she had had her coming-out, Elizabeth had declared that she *would* be independent and it had been with a certain sense of relief that Amelia had argued the cause for her.

"The time must come when she should be allowed to make her own mistakes, Mama," she had said. "She may not make as many as you seem to anticipate. Besides, I do not want her to resent me."

But Lady Didright had refused to admit that the time had come for her to cease to depend on her elder daughter to regulate the behavior of the younger.

"If she would listen to me it might be different," she had protested. "But you know, my dear, she will not. Why, she never has! And now you are proposing that she listen to no one except Randolph who can be depended on to give her all the wrong advice."

Now that the matter had come to a head over the visit to Vauxhall Gardens, Amelia found herself inclined to take her grandfather's advice. Some way must be found to convince her mother that she could no longer be depended on to be the heart and soul of common sense. And Elizabeth must realize that her older sister was no longer prepared to be her watchdog. If she were to go along on the outing and turn a blind eye to any indiscretion Elizabeth cared to make, she might make her point. But when Amelia declared herself ready to make up one of the party, Elizabeth was thrown into a fit of sulks.

"You know you would not enjoy it!" she exclaimed, turning away from the pier glass where she had been admiring herself in her new gown of pink and white striped taffeta. "Besides, I should always feel that you were watching me and that would be quite unendurable. I expect Mama asked you to do it."

Amelia was so accustomed to keeping her temper at all costs in order to maintain peace in the family, that she found herself making the effort now.

"I think it sounds amusing," she replied, picking up a petticoat which Elizabeth had discarded on the floor. "And, as for watching you, I am tired of doing so."

Elizabeth threw her lower lip out in a pout. "You only say that to put me off my guard," she said. "You have never wanted me to have any fun. If you come to Vauxhall with us, you will spoil everything."

But Randolph took a different slant. A cheerful, agreeable young gentleman, two years older than Elizabeth, he had been spoiled and catered to by his mother with no greater damage being done than that he expected life to be a festive board from which he could fill his plate as he pleased.

"You are only being selfish, Beth," he declared when he joined his two sisters in the little sitting room which was between their bedchambers. "Of course you must come to Vauxhall, Amelia. I would have asked you straight away if I had thought you would be interested. The Prince is a jolly fellow and the Duchess of Devonshire will make an admirable duenna for she loves a lark as well now as she did when she was twenty. She and the Prince are great friends and she will brook no criticism of him."

"I do not want to hear about the duchess, Randolph," Elizabeth declared. "Or the Prince either, for that matter. Amelia only wants to go along so that she can offer me advice on my decorum, although she claims the contrary."

Randolph stretched out in the wing chair until his long legs in their buckskin knee breeches and Hessian boots stretched half way across the carpet. Like Elizabeth he was fair and had the same blue eyes, but unlike her he was always cheerful.

"If you want my opinion," he said, clasping his hands over his embroidered waistcoat, "I think that Amelia would find it a relief to pay as little attention to you as possible. Mama has put the responsibility on her of keeping you in line for far too long as it is. Why, I believe that Amelia would have been put in charge of me as well if Mama had thought that I would listen to anything that anyone advised me."

"You make a great show of being more impossible to deal with than you really are," Amelia told her brother with a smile.

"And you are an observant miss!" Randolph replied, blowing her a kiss. "The fact is, you *will* come with us to Vauxhall. Elizabeth is only afraid that you will distract Darrow's attention from her. Her prettiness is one thing, but you have—yes, you have hidden fires! I have always thought it."

"What a great tease you are!" Amelia declared, passing behind his chair for the express purpose of rumpling his hair. "And who is this Darrow who must not be distracted?"

"Oh, you are impossible! Both of you! I declare I cannot bear to be in the same room with either one of you!" Elizabeth announced and took a flounced departure.

"Darrow?" Randolph said reflectively, pretending not to notice that anything out of the way had happened. "I could say he is a young marquess and that would be true enough. I could say that he is handsome and breaks hearts in all directions. I could say that he is the Prince's boon companion and that he makes fun when he cannot find it. But he is more than all that. I think that you must see him to understand. He was at Lady Buttwell's soirée the other evening, having just returned from Paris. That was where our little sister caught his eye. I fancy that you did not see him because Mama kept you in the whist room. You know, of course, that you should not allow it."

Amelia did not trouble to pretend that she did not know what he meant.

"Mama puts great store on beating Mrs. Travice," she replied, "and she wanted me as partner."

Randolph pulled her down on the arm of the chair, and would not release her hand. "Mama has a grand scheme, Amelia," he said with as much gravity as he was capable of showing. "She wants to keep you with her always, I think. That is one reason she begs you to keep a watch on Beth. Certainly that explains why she gave you such a short time in London at your coming-out. She would like to depend on you for everything forever."

"Whatever gave you such a quaint idea?" Amelia said with a laugh which hesitated and failed. "I know. You have been listening to Grandpapa. That is precisely the sort of thing that he would say."

"Mama harps against him so that I believe we all have come to feel that he should not be heeded," Randolph replied, dangling his watchchain to amuse Amelia's tabby cat who had just then leaped down from the sunny window seat and come to join them. "But the fact is, he is astute when it comes to city matters."

"Astute is not quite the same thing as knowledgeable," Amelia replied. "And I think you meant the latter. I cannot think him wise if even one half the stories he tells us of his past are true."

"Ah ha!" Randolph exclaimed, pointing one finger at her. "There you go being sensible! Truly you must cure yourself, Amelia."

"That is very much what Grandpapa told me not an hour ago," she murmured, taking the cat up in her arms and burying her face in its soft black and orange fur.

"You make a pretty picture," her brother told her. "Tell me, why is it you do not make a deal more of your looks? I mean to say, Elizabeth always seems to be having more new gowns made, but you wear the same day after day. And why is it you favor colors that are so subdued? And since it is the latest style to draw the hair up high, why do you wear a *dormeuse?*"

Releasing the tabby, Amelia turned to the round glass which hung above the mantel. It was true that her thick dark curls were nearly hidden by the white cap with its loosely-fitting crown and lace wings trimmed with a blue ribbon which matched her gown. As for the rest, there was nothing about her *polonaise* to attract attention. Small hoop, covered with flounces and furbelows. Skirt short enough to show the ankles. A tulle neckerchief to cover the décolletage provided by the cut of the bodice. A stomacher which showed her slim waist to advantage. All in style but not in advance of it. An ordinary pattern and a color which did nothing to excite.

"You know plain blues and greens suit you best,my dear," her mother would often say. Suddenly Amelia realized that it was not only in a single way that her mother, through constant repetition since she was a child, had made her believe that she would live and dress in a certain way, be a certain kind of person. And, yes, what Randolph had suggested might be right. Certainly her mother had made no secret of having used her to control Elizabeth for years. Now perhaps she had decided that it would be to her advantage if her elder daughter did not marry but instead remained to be her companion and act as a buffer between her and her father.

"Yes," she murmured to herself. "What a fool I may have been."

And yet she knew that she could not change overnight. In fact, she must face the possibility that she could not change at all. Furthermore, was she quite certain that she cared to change or that she would care for the group which surrounded the young Prince, young gentlemen like Darrow who Randolph apparently admired for all the wrong sort of reasons? Even now her brother, whose mind never lingered long on any serious topic, was telling her a rambling story about a recent escapade involving the Prince, his boon companion, Hanger, and a wager based upon a race between a pack of twenty turkeys against twenty geese.

"The Prince laid a deal of cash upon the turkeys," Randolph went on, grinning broadly. "Five hundred pounds, they tell me. This was before we came up to London, you understand, or I would have placed a bet or two of my own. Hanger's a shrewd chap."

Amelia pretended to continue to observe her image closely in the glass in order to keep her back turned to her brother. Were these the sort of stories with which his friends entertained each other to exclusion of all else? she wondered. And would Randolph be tempted to imitate the Prince as to gambling? She gave a little laugh and shook her head as she realized suddenly that she was doing precisely what she had said she would not do. Her brother was telling a simple story which, no doubt, he meant to amuse her, and she was busy thinking of the possible unfortunate circumstances which were implicit in it.

"And which did Mr. Hanger back?" she asked, forcing herself to make a show of interest. "The turkeys or the geese? I should have thought the length of the course would make the difference."

"Dash it, nothing escapes you, does it?" Randolph declared, looking up at her with admiration in his eyes. "No doubt, you've figured it out already. The course was ten miles."

"The month?"

"October."

"The time of day the race commenced?"

"Why, it was early evening."

Amelia smiled. "Then if Mr. Hanger is as shrewd as you say, he backed the geese for, although the turkeys would be faster, they must have flown up into the trees to roost the moment it was dark."

"Just so!" Randolph cried, jumping to his feet. "The Prince was taken in, you understand. They say he made a pretty sight setting at the turkeys with his pole when they began to stretch their necks toward the branches. Why, he and Berkeley even threw barley on the road to lure them down but to no avail."

"I take it that the Prince paid off his debts," Amelia said in a low voice.

"Of course he did," Randolph said on his way to the sitting room door, the tabby close behind him. "He lost the bet."

"But it was no real contest," Amelia argued. "Except, perhaps, of knowledge. The Prince did not happen to know that turkeys roost at night.

There is no reason why he should be wise in country matters. Surely he felt disobliged when he discovered . . ."

"Look at yourself!" her brother interrupted, taking her by the shoulders and whirling her around until she faced the mirror once again. "See, you are frowning like Mama. There was nothing really wrong in what Hanger did and the Prince roared with laughter over it."

"I should have thought the loss of five hundred pounds . . ."

"The Prince cares little for money, although his father is constantly after him to be more frugal," Randolph said. "And no doubt he *is* extravagant. Extravagant *and* frivolous. He does not hold up everything to the window of reason. But he knows how to be merry and there are worse aims in life. Who would you rather be, Mama downstairs, worrying about anything she can find to fret about, or Grandpapa, sitting with old Queensberry staring through their quizzing glasses at the young ladies passing while they recollect old times?"

"Why, as for that," Amelia said, laughing, "I would prefer to be neither."

But Randolph's point had been taken and Amelia made herself a promise that at Vauxhall she would find nothing to condemn and everything to admire.

Chapter 3

Amelia's first impression of Vauxhall Gardens was one of colored lights hanging from the trees making a fairy-land out of broad stretches of walks and carefully trimmed shrubbery. Music was coming from the white pavilion to the right and ladies and gentlemen clustered about tables where they could be served wine and sweets. Wherever she looked couples promenaded and from the shrubbery there came the sound of high-pitched giggles.

They had arrived in three carriages, all showing the Prince's seal. Amelia, Randolph and Elizabeth had been joined in their barouche by the clever gamester, the Honorable George Hanger, and his sister, a pert young lady who wore her powdered hair very high and, after demanding that everyone was to call her Lucy, kept up such a steady stream of chatter that it had been impossible for anyone else to talk.

Now, tearing her eyes away from the brightly-lighted scene, Amelia considered the remainder of the party to whom Randolph had introduced her as soon as they had arrived. The Prince of Wales was rather above the average size, a handsome enough gentleman with strong features and gray eyes who professed himself delighted to meet Randolph's "other sister." With him was the Duchess of Devonshire who was distinguished by the height of her wig and the shrillness of her laughter. A gentleman named Lord Berkeley struck an ominous note on account of a singularly low forehead and glistening eyes which lingered so long on Amelia that she was uncomfortable.

The last member of the party was a certain Lord Darrow, the marquess of whom Randolph had spoken in such glowing terms. Lord Darrow was tall and broad-shouldered and dressed far more casually that the other gentlemen who sported satin frock coats and pantaloons as was usual for evening wear. But the marquess was outfitted in a riding jacket of bottle-blue together with top boots and buckskin breeches. That, at least, was what Amelia noticed first, disconcerted as she was by her encounter with Lord Berkeley.

Now, when she turned away from the lights, she noted that Lord Darrow was handsome in the classic manner with faultless features which might have graced a statue by Praxiteles. And yet there was nothing stiff and detached about him as he stood bantering with the Prince and, when he laughed, it was an infectious sound. Particularly for Elizabeth, it seemed, for she kept her blue eyes riveted on the gentleman and indicated her amusement by a constant stream of giggles, all of which Lord Darrow did not seem to notice.

"It would do no good at all for me to offer your sister advice," her grandpapa had said that afternoon when he had returned from visiting his friend, Old Queensberry. "She's like your mother although I doubt she would admit it. Set on having her way at all costs. But it's a pleasure to tell you what I think you ought to do. I told Q about your predicament, mind you. 'My eldest granddaughter is too good for her own good,' I said. That made him laugh."

Amelia had dryly confessed to being glad she could offer someone some amusement, even secondhand. The thought of two old roués sitting in a bow window facing Piccadilly distracting themselves by discussing her problems had no particular appeal but she knew that she must suffer the consequences of having been so frank with her grandfather that morning. He had promised his advice and now she had little choice but to listen to it.

Unfortunately her grandfather was rarely direct about anything, and she was forced to listen to a certain amount of gossip about "Old Q" before hearing how she was to be advised. With his cane propped between his spindly legs, the old man made a recitation of his friend's latest fads, most of which concerned his health.

"Taking milk baths, he is," her grandfather

declared with a thin smile with the dizzying effect of setting the network of lines in his face into new and extraordinary conjunctions. "Has his man fill a tin tub up to the brim with it."

When Amelia had suggested that it could scarcely do the old man any harm, her grandfather countered with his opinion that it would do him little good.

"Damme if I don't admire him for putting up a good fight," he continued. "Deaf in one ear, you know. One glass eye. But he's a clever fellow. Gives his doctor an annuity of five hundred a year as long as the fellow can keep him alive. Bit of motivation that, eh? Bit of motivation!"

This recitation continued for so long that Amelia was beginning to think she might be spared advice after all, but finally her grandfather came to the point.

"Queensberry agrees with me that you should attend to ruining your reputation as soon as possible," he told her, whereupon Amelia protested that she had not thought of going quite that far.

"I only want not to be considered quite so very sensible by Mama," she said.

"Might as well be hung for a sheep as a goat," Lord Wellingham declared. "Have yourself a bit of fun in the process. Attach yourself to the wrong sort of fellow. That's the ticket! 'Old Q' said he wished he was young enough to oblige!"

There were times, Amelia thought, when she understood something of her mother's frustrations. Certainly it was true that her grandfather was a scandalous, old man with not a shred of caution about him. Still, as she dressed with the help of her abigail that evening, Amelia thought there might be something to his suggestion. It could do no harm, certainly, if she should flirt a bit with someone she was certain her mother would not approve. Certainly the gentlemen the Prince surrounded himself with would provide her with an ample choice.

But now that the moment had come, now that she was actually at Vauxhall, Amelia found she could not steel herself for that particular task. The Duchess of Devonshire's archness provided her with an example she did not wish to emulate, and certainly she would feel a fool to be caught out giggling and preening herself as Elizabeth and the Honorable Lucy Hanger were doing.

And then, quite suddenly, the situation resolved itself without her making any effort. Lord Darrow was presenting his arm to her as couples paired in preparation for a promenade. Amelia saw the outrage in her sister's eyes as she was made Lord Berkeley's companion. The duchess led the way with the Prince and Randolph and the Honorable Lucy Hanger followed, with her brother setting off on his own in order to claim a table.

Amelia had thought that the presence of the heir to the throne would cause a certain sensation once he was recognized, but such was not the case. By way of making conversation, she mentioned to Lord Darrow that she found this most unusual.

"Prinny is a familiar face here," he replied with a smile. "He prides himself on being the most democratic of men, you know, Miss Didright. To his father's displeasure, I might add. We all are classified as scoundrels in the King's book, I fear. Hanger, particularly, but I pride myself in thinking that I run a close second."

Such a frank admission put Amelia at something of a loss. What possible response was there to make to such an extraordinary comment?

"And how does one go about qualifying oneself to be a scoundrel in the King's eyes?" she replied. "Is it a very difficult thing to do?"

She saw that she had disconcerted him. The glance he threw her was a puzzled one.

"I had thought a giggle would have been your response, Miss Didright," he replied.

"It was a joke, sir?"

There was a moment's pause. "I expect I meant it to be one," he said slowly. "But the fact is, it is the truth. You are an extraordinary young lady, Miss Didright. Do you always go about speaking what you think quite so directly?"

Now it was Amelia's turn to be confused. She told herself that this was the proof of the pudding. Certain habits were too deeply engrained. She *was* too serious. And it seemed she could not help it. Given the perfect opportunity to play the flirt, she had been frank and forthright. No doubt Lord Darrow would take advantage of the first opportunity to settle her with the Honorable George Hanger. And who could blame him since she must seem to him to be ready to subject him to an inquisition?

But, instead, when the others chose that moment to settle at a table in one of the alcoves of the pavilion, Lord Darrow suggested that he and she walk a bit further on down the brightly-lighted path which circled the garden. Elizabeth's blue eyes blazed angrily as he made an announcement to that effect.

"I doubt my sister will enjoy it," she was heard to say as Amelia and Lord Darrow turned away. "She is not fond of frivolity, you understand, and would not have come tonight had my mother not wanted her to serve as my chaperone."

"And is that what you are, Miss Didright?" Lord Darrow demanded as they passed the pavilion where, on a balcony, an orchestra was tuning up. "Are you, in fact, your sister's chaperone? It seems an odd role for one so young and beautiful."

"You are too kind, sir," Amelia murmured in some confusion. "Elizabeth was amusing herself at my expense, perhaps. It is a way that sisters often have."

They had turned to take another path which led down to the river. The colored lights cast their reflection in the water. The crush was not so great here and the perfume in the air came from the flowers which were planted in thick borders rather than from the mingling of scores of artificial scents.

"I think that it is true that frivolity does not amuse you, however," Lord Darrow murmured.

It occurred to Amelia that she should not answer him as frankly as she might have done in other circumstances. Perhaps she had not begun as a flirt, but that did not mean she could not end the evening as one. Her grandfather had suggested that she form an attachment to someone her mother would find unsuitable. It followed that since Lord Darrow was part of the Prince of Wales' entourage he would earn instant disapproval in her mother's eyes. Further, if she were to flirt, Elizabeth's anger would know no bounds. She would be certain to speak of it at home and Amelia would have gained her desired end of not being sensible with very little trouble.

The more she thought of it the more feasible the idea sounded. If Lord Darrow had been someone other than he was, she might have had to fear that, once encouraged, he would pursue her. But clearly he was accustomed to more sophisticated ladies and handsome and carefree as he was, he doubtless could have his choice of any partner he preferred. Tonight, the company being limited, he had chosen her. But she was certain that he would forget her existence once the evening ended. The only necessary thing was that she should seem attracted to him and wait for Elizabeth to make her report.

"Perhaps I have been impertinent," she heard the marquess say as they turned back toward the pavilion. "Although, I confess, it has been my experience that ladies like to be asked about themselves."

"Perhaps I am not like most ladies of your acquaintance, sir," Amelia replied pertly, hoping that she struck the right tone.

"You are an enigma, Miss Didright," he confessed and now he was no longer smiling. "One moment you are frank, and arch the next."

Amelia told herself that it would be wise for

them to join the others as soon as possible. Safely in a group, she could express her admiration for the gentleman with less chance of having her sincerity questioned. Lord Darrow might be the scoundrel he called himself but she thought her brother had been closer to the truth when he had indicated that he did not care to place the gentleman in a category. She thought herself that the young marquess was more complex than he cared to admit. Certainly he was extraordinarily sensitive. How quickly he had called her out when she had changed her course in midstream.

"I do believe the orchestra is playing now," she said, speeding her steps. "Yes, I can hear the tune quite plainly now. Do you think there will be singing, Lord Darrow? And fireworks? I have never been here before, you know. No doubt you and the Prince come often."

She did not stop talking until they were safely back with the others. The little group was cheerful enough for the claret had been passed around the gentlemen, and the ladies sipped ratafia, a light liquor flavored with fruit kernels and bitter almonds. Elizabeth moved her seat to put the table between her and Lord Berkeley and declared that Amelia and Lord Darrow had not been gone long.

"But then, I expect my sister found a good deal to disapprove of," she continued.

"Young ladies should not make judgments, I often say," the Duchess of Devonshire observed, patting her pinnacle of powdered hair. "After all, they have so very little to base them on. Do you not agree, Prinny? Come! You must support me."

Amelia felt her face grow hot. There had been no need for Elizabeth to have made her the center of attention in this way. She was only taking her revenge for the fact that Lord Darrow had not given her his full attention.

The Prince declared that he knew very little about what young ladies should or should not do and Hanger pounded himself on the knee and shouted that that was the greatest nonsense he had ever heard. The informality with which the Prince was treated continued to amaze Amelia but she reminded herself that she must pass no judgments. Aware that Lord Darrow was watching her curiously, she gave herself up to listening to the music. Later she could confide in Randolph that she found Lord Darrow most attractive with the certainty that he would let Elizabeth know.

And so Amelia decided on her course, knowing that she took the coward's way. When the fireworks began exploding in great red and golden balls above the river, Elizabeth and the Honorable Lucy Hanger screamed and clutched Lord Darrow's arms. Amelia knew that, at the very least, she should do the same. But she did not dare because he had shown himself too clever. If he had found her archness false, what would he think if she were to make a great pretense of being startled by the explosions?

At evening's end, however, she favored him with a smile. Elizabeth had manipulated things in such a way that it was Lord Darrow and Berkeley who accompanied them back in the carriage rather than the two Honorable Hangers, and had made herself the center of attention. When they reached the house on Portman Square, however, Lord Darrow got down from the side of the carriage where he and Amelia both had been sitting and offered her assistance in her descent.

"I cannot determine whether you enjoyed the evening or not, Miss Didright," he murmured. "But I assure you that I hope you did."

That was when Amelia smiled and, perhaps because it required no artifice to do so, she felt a sudden rush of happiness. The glow of it must have lingered on her face for when they were inside the house and the footman had closed the door behind them, Elizabeth took one look at Amelia and gave a little cry.

"You fancy him!" she declared in a high, shrill voice. "I knew you would! Oh, it's just as I predicted. You've ruined everything!"

Chapter 4

"**Damme, it's like you not to waste any time, my dear!**" Lord Wellingham announced when Amelia entered the morning room. The sun was streaming through the long window which led out into a tiny garden and the fragrance of warm bread was in the air. Roses decorated the table and, when Amelia bent to kiss her grandfather, the old man leaned forward to pull a yellow bloom from the vase and present it to her in a gallant manner which hinted at the dandy he had been in his youth.

"You have my congratulations," he continued, his wizened face further bent and twisted by a smile. "Mind, I do not know the ins and outs of it as yet but Elizabeth is closeted with your mama in the blue salon and, if these old ears are any judge, she is making some complaint about your behavior at Vauxhall last night. The name of Darrow was mentioned, I believe."

And with that he began to cackle as though he were very well pleased with himself indeed.

Amelia pressed the rose to her cheek and closed her eyes. What a pity everything could not remain as calm and beautiful as this moment. And yet it had been her desire to maintain harmony which had led her to allow her mother to take advantage of her. She had decided to change her life and she must take the consequences, willy-nilly. Elizabeth might complain to their mama all she liked, but, if she pleased, Amelia could remain outside the quarrel. The main thing was that she no longer be considered the bulwark of common sense on which the entire family could depend.

"No doubt you'll wonder how I could have heard that much," her grandfather announced as Amelia poured herself a cup of tea. "Damme if I didn't listen at the door! Don't know how long a time it's been since I was up to a prank like that. Not a doubt in the world that it's done me a deal of good to be in London again. Scandal! Intrigue! Thankee, my dear, for bringing a bit of both into the house. Not that your brother and sister wouldn't have done so, given the time, but I'll count on you to make a better job of it. I'll be a muckworm if I won't!"

Amelia suppressed a sigh with difficulty. Clearly her grandfather intended to make as much as possible of any new excitement. As for what it was precisely that Elizabeth was telling her mother, she could not be certain for the night before, having delivered herself of her outburst in the hall, her sister had clutched up her skirts and hurried up the stairs. When Amelia had come into the sitting room they shared, it was to find the door to her bedchamber closed and her abigail waiting to say that her other mistress had retired with a migrim.

She had told herself she did not care. Elizabeth was spoiled. There was no question of that. And she was selfish. Never once did she consider Amelia's happiness. Thanks to their mother's influence, she had come to think of her sister as someone who thought of nothing but how to make life more comfortable for others. Amelia was there to keep her out of scrapes, to mop up the proverbial spilled milk. And when, just once, Amelia had made it clear that she might enjoy her own self without consideration of any other person, when she had committed such a simple act of folly as to have been gracious to Lord Darrow, Elizabeth had flown into a fury.

For a moment, remembering his eyes as the young marquess had said good night to her the evening before, Amelia started to forget that it had all been a charade on her part in order to disenchant her mother. And, even though it meant unpleasantness, Elizabeth was doing precisely what Amelia had hoped that she would do. No doubt she was painting her sister's behavior in the most terrible colors imaginable even though she would have to stretch the truth to do so. And, as for Lord Darrow . . .

It came to Amelia suddenly that there was a

chance for error in her plan. If Elizabeth had her own eye on the marquess, she would not want to picture him as any sort of rake. The consequence might be that Elizabeth's reputation would be tarnished to no greater extent than was attendant on her playing the jade.

That would not do. She saw that at once and clearly. And yet how could she admit in one breath to her mother that she had flirted with the gentleman and, in the next, declare him to be a scoundrel? She raised her eyes and found her grandfather munching a bun in his own unique and toothless way.

"Grandpapa," Amelia said slowly. "I wonder if you would care to do me a favor?"

Lord Wellingham did not attempt to hide his enthusiasm. No doubt, had he been more spry, he would have leaped to his feet. As it was he took up his cane and beat a rapid tattoo on the floor.

"Damme, it would be a pleasure, gel!" he declared in his creaking voice. "Nothing is too much to ask, mind!"

Amelia drew her chair closer to his and lowered her voice to a whisper. "I don't suppose you happen to know Lord Darrow?" she inquired.

"One of the Prince of Wales's friends," the old man said promptly. "Queensberry and I don't let ourselves get out of touch, you know. Don't tell me you've decided to take up with the fellow! Dash it, I knew I could depend on you, my dear."

"I do not intend to 'take up' with anyone, Grandpapa," Amelia replied. "But I want Mama to think that I have a penchant for someone she thinks unsuitable and I believe Lord Darrow might qualify."

"Cock of the walk from what I hear," the old man told her. "Splendid fellow! After my heart! That sort of thing. The very image of me when I was younger. Take my word on it, he's the sort of fellow you ought to marry. Someone with a spark of life. Pity your grandmother isn't with us still, God bless her soul. Gave her any amount of pleasure to think she'd tamed me, you know."

"Then will you tell Mama that you think Lord Darrow is very much what you were before you married?" Amelia asked him. "That should serve the purpose very well, I think."

Lord Wellingham hoisted himself from the chair with as much alacrity as he was capable of, all the time proclaiming that nothing would suit him better, a declaration which he accompanied with a number of colorful oaths of the sort which would have made his daughter blanch had she been present. Even Elizabeth, who chose that moment to enter the room, looked properly askance, but she recovered herself at once and addressed Amelia in a triumphant fashion.

"I have told Mama all about your sad behavior last night," she said, "and she wants to see you in the blue salon at once."

And with that thrust she whirled out of the room, skirts flying.

"I'll see her first, gel," Lord Wellingham declared, propelling himself into the corridor with his cane. "Damme, I'll tell her Darrow is just the sort of fellow I'd choose for you myself."

"And what was that about?" Randolph demanded as he narrowly avoided being knocked down by his grandfather. "What sort of bee has the old rumstick got in his noggin now?"

"You would do better to show the proper respect," Amelia said sharply. Granted that she had set events in motion, but now she was not so certain that she liked the way that they were going.

"I only know that something has gone awry," Randolph replied, helping himself to a spoonful of jelly. "First Elizabeth nearly topples me down the stairs in her hurry to get up them and now my own grandfather tries to knock me down as well. What's more, I'll be a gudgeon if I didn't hear him mention Darrow."

"I may have mentioned him," Amelia said carefully, going to the window and looking out at the tiny garden. Roses hugged the weathered brick wall and snapdragons tangled their pink and yellow heads together. It made her think of the country and she found herself wishing she were back there. London was all very well but life was complicated here, at best. What she had tried to do had seemed so simple when she had conceived it but now she felt, somehow, that she was treading a precarious path which might lead her somewhere she had not intended.

"Dashed fine fellow, Darrow," Randolph continued, making a great clank and clatter of the cutlery and china. "And I think he took a fancy to you. All of which makes quite a change since the usual way of things is that young ladies tend to throw themselves at him."

"Well, then," Amelia said more sharply than she had intended, "it is easy to see why he fancies himself so. In my opinion . . ."

She paused just in time to remind herself that she must show a certain consistency to her family in regard to her impression of Lord Darrow. If, as she intended, her mother was to think that she admired him excessively, she must not put Randolph in the way of dropping some comment which would indicate just the reverse.

"In my opinion," she continued in a milder tone, "he is a most appealing gentleman."

" 'Pon my soul!" Randolph exclaimed. "You like him, then! Now that's a whizwhee if I ever heard one!"

"Mind," Amelia said in sudden alarm, "you must say nothing to him."

"No doubt he will want to have a word or two with me," Randolph replied, with a teasing smile. "And so, we are to make you one of us at last."

"I do not know what you mean by that," Amelia said primly. "Indeed, I seem to have made Elizabeth shake her feathers and Mama is asking for an interview. Everyone is behaving in a singularly odd way."

"But that is only because you are not acting like yourself," her brother told her, winking one eye suggestively. "Mind you, Grandpapa told me you had hidden depths, but even so . . ."

"The less you talk to our grandfather the better," Amelia reported just as the old gentleman in question made his way back into the room.

"I seem to have done a deal of trouble," Lord Wellingham announced with a great show of dignity, despite the fact that his periwig had toppled sideways on his head. "I had no sooner told your mama that I completely approved of your choice of Darrow than she fell into such a temper that I was forced to call the footman to bring her salts. But, even so, she insists on seeing you, my dear. And, damme, she is in a temper!"

For once, as Amelia was shortly to discover, her grandfather had been guilty of understatement for, when she entered the blue salon, she found her mother in a state of near distraction, darting first one way and then the next like a demented sparrow.

"What do you mean?" she demanded somewhat illogically, pausing to rap a table with her folded fan. "What do you mean? I will not have it! Do you understand! I will not have it!"

"Pray calm yourself, Mama," Amelia said. "I do not like to see you in such a state. Allow me to fetch your vinaigrette."

"So it is true then!" Lady Didright exclaimed, dropping onto the settee, only to hop up again as though the cushions were red-hot. "You do not deny it! Oh, dear! Oh, dear! What have I done to deserve it!"

Amelia was not a monster and she did not like to see her mother suffer. It was necessary for her to remind herself that her own survival was at stake here. If she were to reassure her mother that there were no grounds for her concern, she would rapidly assume her old persona and become once again the practical, sensible, dependable Amelia whose fate it might well be to remain her mother's companion for life. All that was necessary was for her to be kept out of the limelight as much as possible for this single Season. Elizabeth was certain to come away from London engaged and she would subsequently marry. Randolph would continue his pursuits. And, once Amelia was safely back in the country, there would be no way that she could return to London or, for that matter, go to Bath or anywhere Society gathered, without her mother for companion. A young and single lady was by way of being a prisoner. She saw that now. And she would not be forced into that position!

"Perhaps you had a mental aberration," Lady Didright said hopefully, coming to a momentary halt before her elder daughter and screwing up her face until her brown eyes nearly met. "I would even be happy to learn that you drank too much ratafia. That was it, my dear, surely! You simply lost your head!"

"Why, what is it that so much concerns you, Mama?" Amelia replied, hating herself for the pretense of innocence but aware that it was necessary.

"How can you ask me? Elizabeth has been to see me already this morning about your behavior last night at Vauxhall. It must have been outrageous indeed if she was flurried, for we all know how giddy she is. I would never have believed that you could stoop to a flirtation with a gentleman like Lord Darrow! You, with all your common sense!"

"Mama," Amelia said quite gently, taking the little woman by the hand and leading her to the settee. "I have no more common sense than any other young girl of my age. You gave me the responsibility of Elizabeth some years ago and have called me sensible so often ever since that I myself came to believe it."

But her attempt to be direct did not prevail. Instead, Lady Didright leaped to her feet and began to dart about again in an aimless manner.

"What are you talking about?" she demanded. "I wish to speak of your behavior with Lord Darrow and you talk of something else completely. I put it to you quite direct, miss. Did you or did you not carry on a flirtation with him?"

Amelia took a deep breath. "If Elizabeth says I did, Mama, then I expect it must be true."

"Even though you knew him to be a bounder?"

"Surely not, Mama. He is one of the Prince's closest friends."

"*That* speaks for itself! And, as though that were not quite enough, your grandfather recommends him! That is all the evidence I need to be certain that the fellow is a scoundrel."

It was unfair, Amelia thought, that Lord Darrow should be so arbitrarily treated but, after all, it scarcely mattered. He would never know that he had been maligned by her mother and, even if he did, he would not care.

"Surely, Mama," Amelia argued, "you would

not have allowed us to go to Vauxhall as part of the Prince's party if you had thought . . ."

"But I *did* think!" Lady Didright exclaimed. "You know I was opposed to it. But I knew that your brother and sister would, no doubt, defy me if I tried to prevent them from going. You know how little influence I have with them. If only your poor father were alive. But, as it is, I have been forced to depend on you. And you have failed me!"

Amelia knew this was the ultimate appeal. Nothing her mother could have said would have made her feel more guilty. No doubt Lady Didright expected that she would respond by admitting she had been wrong and pledge to return to her former position of being her mother's agent. But this, Amelia steadfastly determined, she would not do.

"I am sorry that you think that, Mama," she declared, raising her chin. "But I have feelings and I confess they have been deeply touched."

It was as delicate and indirect a comment as she could make under the circumstances, but it was quite sufficient to send her mother darting from the room, holding her turbaned head in both hands as though she expected it to spin away.

"I cannot think what I shall do!" Amelia heard her cry. "Dear me! Dear me! I shall surely lose my mind!"

Chapter 5

It was not in Lady Didright's scheme of things, however, that she should ever lose anything without a struggle, including Amelia's continued support and assistance which was, no doubt, the reason that the Duchess of Bradlaw appeared at the house on Portman Square that very afternoon.

To say that the duchess possessed an aggressive, masterful, overpowering, not to mention offensive personality would be an understatement. Even her friends, of whom she had very few, were able to say very little in her defense for, in addition to those attributes already mentioned, she was arrogant, unkind, and totally without scruple when it came to getting her own way. There was nothing she liked better than a family squabble and, since she had not been blessed with children

it was necessary for her to resort to others for
family problems to solve and she could frequently
be heard to declare that, if it were not for her,
London would be resounding with the news of
domestic disasters on every side. According to the
duchess, she had returned any number of erring
husbands to their hearths, turned spendthrift sons
into models of propriety and subdued defiant
daughters by the scores. Armed with this self-
proclaimed reputation, she marched into Lady
Didright's drawing room with all the assurance of
Alexander the Great approaching Persia.

"Good afternoon, my dear Selina," she said in
her gruff voice. "I came as soon as I received your
letter. There, there. Never fear. We will soon put
things straight. Why, if one's elder daughter cannot be depended on, I cannot think who can."

The duchess' physique was as overwhelming as
her personality. A tall, broad-bosomed lady of
middle age, she wore her sacque gown as though
it were a uniform and even managed something
military in the effect created by her extraordinarily large hat which was shaped like a beehive
and fitted over the top of her towering coiffure.
Her face, as well, might have become a soldier for
she had the same thrusting nose and bulging eyes
so often seen on ancient statuary. To see her and
tiny Lady Didright embrace was to be amazed
that one could be so vast and the other quite so
tiny. Indeed, Randolph had once irreverently declared that, when he saw them together he was
reminded of an elephant and that wee bird which
makes a habit of traveling on the other's back.

The Duchess of Bradlaw had a good many opinions and, given the opportunity, was more than willing to give them an airing. In line with this, she lost no time in telling Lady Didright that, although she had not liked to interfere before, not having been asked to do so, she had long since thought that this particular household was not being run at all as it ought.

"In the first place, there is the matter of your father, my dear Selina," she declared, situating herself in the Chippendale armchair and impaling her hostess with a sharp glance. "It is a perfect scandal that he is allowed to sit with Queensberry in that bow window in full sight of everyone and behave like a young blood of eighteen. No doubt he is in his dotage, which makes it all the more imperative that he be confined to this house. Indeed, that is my first recommendation!"

With that she made it clear that she had been called in to take the reins of the entire household out of Lady Didright's hands, figuratively speaking, and, when Her Ladyship puckered her face and said that keeping her father inside might prove unduly difficult, the duchess announced that surely something might be made of the fact that gadding about London must constitute a danger to his health.

"La, I have always been relieved that both my parents departed this world before they became an embarassment to me," she continued, sitting very straight and tall in her chair. The duchess was a stout woman and sat with her feet apart in such a way as to make even the fullness of her silk skirts strain at the seams.

To do her justice, Lady Didright announced that, although her father was often a nuisance and an embarrassment, she loved him dearly and did not want him dead, to which the duchess responded with an unpleasant sort of hoot to indicate disbelief, at which Lady Didright was quite effectively silenced.

"Now, let us consider Randolph," the duchess continued. "He would much better take up the company of some respectable young Tories, you know. The King prefers them to the Whigs who are the Prince's friends."

"But surely it will be more to Randolph's ultimate advantage . . ."

"You are thinking of the time when the King is dead and the Prince of Wales has taken his place. Whom of us is to know how far distant that time may be? The King is in excellent health once more and, unlike his son, he does not dissipate. Furthermore, it is quite possible that the Prince will create a situation soon in which he cannot hope to be accepted by the nicest people such as myself."

"Whatever can you mean, Dorelle?" Lady Didright demanded, assuming one of her many customary masks of terror.

"It is not common gossip yet," the duchess replied in a strong, penetrating voice, "but the Prince is being most unwise. You may have met a certain young widow called Mrs. Fitzherbert."

"Indeed, I do not think . . ."

"She is not as young as the Prince, mind, but

she is far from being long in the tooth. And widowed not once but twice! However, that is not the most distressing feature of the affair."

"Affair!" Lady Didright exclaimed. "Affair!"

"Actually, I do not think it has come to that as yet," the duchess told her. "As it happens, Mrs. Fitzherbert is reputed to be singularly virtuous. No, the fact is that she is Catholic which, of course, puts her beyond the pale completely as far as the royal family is concerned."

"But of course!" Lady Didright cried for, although she was not a highly educated woman, she knew enough of the history of her country to realize the present impossibility of such an alliance as the duchess was hinting at.

"There are some who whisper that he intends to marry her," her friend went on with the air of one whose tongue drips liquid gold. "If that becomes the case, I would not care to have *my* son, should I have had one, associated with someone prepared to bring disgrace upon the royal family."

Lady Didright's eyes appeared about to pop out of her face at this disclosure. "Oh dear!" she whispered. "This is worse than I imagined."

"Things usually are, my dear," the duchess told her. "At least, that has been my experience."

"But what can I do about Randolph?" Lady Didright demanded. "I cannot force *him* to stay at home."

The duchess smiled a wicked smile. "He is dependent on you still for an allowance, I think," she murmured.

Not for the first time Lady Didright marveled at the amount of information her friend possessed.

"He inherited his knighthood, of course," she said, "but I implored his father to be cautious as to the financial end of things and Randolph does not come into the full estate until he is twenty-one. Money is dispensed at my discretion, as a consequence."

"How very wise," the duchess said approvingly. "Nothing could be simpler then. Without funds, he can do nothing. You are in a position to choose his friends for him, I think."

"Randolph will be very angry," his mother said with a shudder. "I cannot bear to think what he will say if I . . ."

The duchess made as though to rise. "If you are not prepared to take my advice," she said, "there is no purpose in further conversation."

"Oh, I will take it!" Lady Didright cried. "Pray continue, dear Dorelle. How shall I manage Elizabeth?"

"Ah, now that *is* an interesting problem," the duchess said, apparently mollified. "She is such an impetuous gel and with a temper to match. She is flighty, I think, and impatient, as well as being . . ."

"*I* should not be so severe on her," Lady Didright interposed.

"Ah, but you are her mother!" the duchess countered. "Mothers can never see their children for what they are. For example, you will pretend that Amelia is rather plain and cares nothing for entertainment. Whereas the truth is quite different if I am to believe the letter which brought me here."

Lady Didright acknowledged that this was so. "It was then that I knew I must have your help, my dear Dorelle. Somehow *I* must be at fault for Amelia's unusual behavior for she really is a quiet girl and prefers to be reserved. Whereas, if I can believe her sister and I think I must, last night she behaved no better than a common jade. It goes without saying that a man like Lord Darrow would have paid no attention to her unless she had thrust herself on him in the most indiscreet sort of manner."

The duchess raised her head and appeared to sniff the air like a hunting hound who scents the fox. "Darrow?" she said. "Hugh Darrow? How does he come into this, pray?"

"It must be that I did not mention him by name in the letters," Lady Didright exclaimed. "La, I was so distraught about my interview with Amelia that I scarcely knew what I was doing!"

The Duchess of Bradlaw took a deep breath and breathed it out again in such a way as to make her considerable bosom more considerable still. "Are you quite certain that your daughter's admirer was Lord Darrow, Selina?" she demanded. "Because I happen to know a great deal about that gentleman."

Lady Didright pulled her eyes together in a worried frown. "I know he must be a great rake," she said in a voice which scarcely rose above a whisper, "because my father recommended him to me. Why, he dared to say that Lord Darrow was just the sort of gentleman he would like to see Amelia married to."

"Then your father is not such a great fool as I have been led to believe," the duchess replied tartly. "Lord Darrow is a prize, Selina. Oh, I will be the first to admit that he runs about in a fast crowd and is a close friend of the Prince. But there are other factors to be considered, my friend, and you would be foolhardy not to do so, prim as you are."

"I do not consider myself excessively prim," Lady Didright said stiffly, looking hurt.

"Let us say that your expectations of how people should behave are not in accordance with the current mores of Society," the duchess replied. "All of which is very admirable, I'm sure. If one has nothing else to congratulate oneself upon, it is a fine thing to be able to speak of one's high level of morality. But that is by-the-by. We were speaking of Lord Darrow. He is rich, Selina. I do not mean mildly rich. I mean that the young gentleman is wealthy."

Lady Didright sneezed delicately into her lace handkerchief. "You know my opinion of money, Dorelle," she replied. "One must have a sufficiency to provide the little comforts of life but more than that brings temptation."

"Twenty thousand pounds a year," the duchess said triumphantly. "He's worth that if he is worth a shilling."

"It appears that you did not hear me, my friend," Lady Didright replied. "Money means little to me."

"I heard you," the duchess said grimly, "and I am not such a fool as to believe what you said. Not only is the young gentleman rich as Croesus, but he is handsome and intelligent, with a sense of humor which is, I always think, such an important thing. But there is one other regard. And it is this. He is cool with young ladies, very. Few of them manage even to attract his passing interest."

Lady Didright, having kept her bird-like restlessness in check for quite as long as she was able, jumped from the chair and began to dart about the room.

"My dear Dorelle," she declared in passing. "All of this is very interesting, I am sure, but I do not know what I am expected to do with the information. I do not wish Amelia to marry . . ."

"Well? You do not want her to marry well?" the duchess cried incredulously. "I have just made it clear to you that she has shown excellent taste in choosing to flirt with Lord Darrow, even if he is a friend of the Prince. Tell me. How did Elizabeth say that he responded. I have seen him put off the advances of young ladies before, some of them greater beauties than Amelia."

"They walked together. At Vauxhall. They were alone for quite half an hour."

The duchess did not trouble to hide her amazement. "I do not believe that I have seen or heard of Darrow spending as much as five minutes with a lady exclusively. Your elder daughter may have never played the flirt before, Selina, but I declare that it would seem she has a natural talent for it. I really think I must advise you to encourage her to carry on. It may well be that the marquess will change his mind about the wedded state."

Lady Didright made a little scuttle to the right and clutched the ornate mahogany trim of the settee.

"I scarcely think . . ." she began.

"There is something you have not told me," the duchess said rising from her chair, the better to tower over her tiny, flustered friend. "Selina, you must be entirely honest with me if I am to help you untangle your affairs. What is it you want for your elder daughter?"

"Well," Lady Didright said, tearing her handkerchief to shreds in her great agitation, "the truth is that Amelia has so much common sense . . ."

"I have heard that litany before," her friend said dryly. "What do you want for her? You know you can be truthful with me."

"I *did* think that it would be very pleasant if, after Elizabeth and Randolph are settled with homes of their own, that Amelia might return to the country with me," Lady Didright confessed. "Of course Randolph and his bride will occupy Random Hall, but there is a charming dower house waiting for me and my father."

She raised her eyes to those of the duchess, although it required that she bend back very far to do so.

"The fact is," she declared, her brown eyes filling with tears, "I cannot bear to think of having the full responsibility of Papa. He will live forever, you know. You might not think it to look at him, but he is in excellent health."

"I am sorry to hear it, my dear," the duchess told her, "but you cannot mean to tell me that you intend Amelia to remain your companion indefinitely!"

"Only until Papa is—no longer with us," Lady Didright said delicately. "Dear Dorelle, will you not sit down? To look at you makes me so very uncomfortable. There. So kind of you. This is what I want to say. I hold no false hopes. You must be quite assured of that."

"By which you mean?"

"Only that if I *have* been mistaken about Amelia and if she *has* set her affection on Lord Darrow, and if he *is* the prize you think him and attracted to her to boot, I doubt that even anyone as clever as you, my dear Dorelle will be able to prevent a marriage."

There was some question among Lady Didright's friends as to whether foolishness was only a clever mask or whether it was precisely what it appeared to be. In this case it was not clear whether she had simply stumbled on the very words which would provide the duchess with a challenge she could not ignore or if she had simply spoken what was on her mind. Perhaps it did not matter since the results were just the same.

"There is certain to be quite a simple solution," the duchess told her. "There is no great trick to separating a naive young lady from her beau. I shall give the matter thought and report to you the moment an idea comes to mind to fit the particular circumstances. In the meantime, pretend to let her have her way. If they appear at the same entertainment, do not attempt to keep them apart. We will be able all the more surely to take them by surprise if they expect no attack."

"How can I ever thank you, my dear Dorelle?" Lady Didright declared.

"Success is its own reward," her friend informed her, making a great todo with her pelisse and reticule preparatory to taking her departure. "Mind what I said about keeping your father inside. He must not continue to make a fool of himself with Queensberry. And make it quite clear to Randolph that you must be satisfied as to whom he makes his friends before you will provide him with funds. I will think about Elizabeth. Silly gels are often awkward to control. But the great thing is Amelia. You will have her in the country with you yet, my friend. You will have her in the country yet!"

Chapter 6

Much to Amelia's relief, her ploy seemed to have been completely successful. Her mother had come to her room following the Duchess of Bradlaw's departure on the pretext of asking for some ribbon, but clearly with the intent of demonstrating that the air was clear after the storm that morning. Not only did she not mention Vauxhall or Lord Darrow, but she did not protest the fact that Amelia and her abigail were at work trimming the pockets of the apron on a polonaise with scarlet ribbon which made a daring effect against the pink gauze with which the evening gown was made.

"Young gels should have a bit of color about their gowns," was her only response as she touched Amelia's curls with a tender gesture and was gone. Elizabeth, who had been standing by the window, waiting to hear Amelia be rebuked, did not trouble to hide her disappointment.

"Mama let you off far too easily!" she exclaimed. "I am surprised she is allowing you to go with us to Lady Featherstone's tonight! I thought that I had made it quite clear to her that your behavior last night was so outrageous . . ."

"Hand me the spool of thread, Doris," Amelia said to her abigail as though they were alone in the room. Formerly, when she had still been convinced that she was sensible and very full of common sense and responsible in good part for maintaining peace in the household, she would have felt it necessary to admonish her sister for her display of temper. Indeed, she guessed that Elizabeth would be well pleased to have her do so now for, although part of her ill nature was based on pique at having been ignored by Lord Darrow last night, another part resulted from a confusion caused by the fact that dependable Amelia was not behaving as she ought.

"I think this red will be very striking," she continued now, holding her needle up to the light. "Do tell me, Doris, shall we gather up the train with a braid or cord?"

"I shall be needing Doris very shortly to do my hair for tonight!" Elizabeth announced. "I do think it is very inconsiderate of you, Amelia, to have monopolized her today when there are any number of things I need to have done for *me*."

"I think I shall be daring and wear one of those padded cork contraptions that fit under the train at the back of the waist," Amelia said to Doris as though her sister had not spoken. "There is just time for you to pop around to Bond Street and buy me one. Here is my reticule. Take what you need out of it."

"Do you mean to say that you intend to wear a false rump?" Elizabeth demanded when Doris had left the room. "Why, I shall go directly to Mama and . . ."

"I should think that you had had quite enough to say to Mama today already," Amelia said cooly. "And, now, if you don't mind, I will just borrow one of your ruffs."

It was considered in the height of fashion that year for ladies to complement an uncovered décolletage with a large double or triple ruff of tulle or gauze with folds of satin added, and Elizabeth had several, one of which was lying on a table just inside her bedchamber. Before her outraged sister could cross the sitting room, Amelia had it and was fitting it about her slender neck. She was wearing a negligée made of white lustring and she looked a pretty sight as she stood before the pier glass with her dark curls hanging on her shoulders. When Elizabeth tried to take the ruff away from her, she simply laughed.

"Turn about is fair enough," she said. "You have borrowed whatever you wanted of mine for years," she told her sister.

Elizabeth stared at her in amazement. "What has come over you?" she demanded. "You have not acted like yourself since last evening."

"And you have behaved even more yourself

than usual," Amelia retorted. "I assure you it has not been a particularly edifying spectacle."

Elizabeth was accustomed to gentle reproofs and cosseting and she was as bewildered as she was outraged. Her mother was behaving in a most peculiar manner and now Amelia could not be anticipated in anything. Unable now to think of a suitable retort, she satisfied herself by stamping her slippered feet against the floor.

"If you are determined to behave as a child," Amelia said, still smiling, "you must be your own audience."

And, scooping up her freshly trimmed gown, she went into her own bedchamber and firmly shut the door.

Once alone, however, she could not maintain her mood or confidence. Hanging the gown in the mahogany wardrobe in the corner, she went to sit on one side of the canopied bed and stared into the middle distance in a distracted manner. She had made just the sort of bold beginning she had hoped to make and Elizabeth's response came as no particular surprise. But she did not know just what to make of her mother's behavior. This morning she had been hysterical but, since her visit with the Duchess of Bradlaw, she appeared to be prepared to hector no longer. Tonight would be the test. Either she would behave as usual, finding excuses to keep Amelia off the dance floor or she would not. Amelia found it difficult to believe that she could have won so easily.

And yet, that evening, when she joined her mother, together with Elizabeth and Randolph in the downstairs hall where they were waiting for the carriage which was to take them to Lady Featherstone's, Lady Didright, although clearly startled by Amelia's appearance, only murmured that she looked very well indeed. Randolph signified his approval by applying his quizzing glass to his eye and drawing a thin whistle between his teeth, while Elizabeth looked sullen and muttered something about *her* ruff.

It was astonishing, Amelia thought, how much difference the clothes she wore could make in the way she felt. Always before, in her plain gowns and white lace cap, she had felt something of a shadow. But tonight, with the train of her pink polonaise gown caught up with red ribbon to form a bustle effect and her décolletage worn low beneath the borrowed ruff, she felt the difference keenly. Doris had dressed her hair high, weaving a string of brilliants among the curls to create a glittering effect.

"Hey ho!" her grandfather declared as he came to join them, arrayed in an old-fashioned dressing gown of faded brocade. "Damme if you don't make a pretty sight, gel! High time, I say. High time!"

He carried a bottle of claret under one arm and Amelia saw her mother's lips tighten. She waited for the explosion which did not come. Instead Lady Didright murmured something about changes to be made and darted out the door as the footman opened it with Elizabeth and Randolph close behind her.

"Darrow is a lucky fellow," her grandfather

announced as he kissed Amelia a fond good-bye. "I'll be a muckworm if he ain't."

The time would come, Amelia knew, when she would have to disillusion him, but for tonight it did no harm to let his imagination run wild. Tomorrow she must warn him not to say a word about the marquess to his friend, Lord Queensberry, however, for she would not care to have a false rumor circulated. In the meantime she would be content with what appeared to be an easily-won freedom.

And, indeed, when they reached Lady Featherstone's fine mansion on Grosvenor Square, Lady Didright did not so much as counsel Amelia to keep a close eye on her sister. Instead, she went straight to the room where whist was being played, leaving her children to their own devices.

There was a considerable crowd in Lady Featherstone's elegant ballroom, most of them people Amelia did not know, but Elizabeth sallied into the room as though it was familiar turf, discarding the sulking she had carried with her in the carriage in an instant, and smiling to right and left quite as though she were royalty.

"No doubt she hopes to discover Darrow somewhere about and corner him to make up for her disappointment last evening," Randolph suggested.

Amelia was startled and she knew she showed it for she saw her brother grin.

"It did not occur to me that he might be here," she said. "Mama thinks highly of Lady Featherstone . . ."

"Dash it, Darrow is welcome everywhere," Randolph told her laughing. "In fact I understand that hostesses vie with one another constantly to get him. Mama may disapprove of the Prince of Wales and his circle, but that is simply because she is so dreadfully proper. I am surprised she made no comment on your gown, and while I am on the subject . . ."

The violins were being tuned in preparation for the first cotillion, but Randolph ushered his sister into a corner. "I want to say this while we are alone," he murmured. "Something is going on."

"I don't know what you mean," Amelia protested. It was unlike Randolph to be so grim.

"Trouble, I think," her brother told her. "I only want you to keep your eyes well peeled. And your ears open. I suspect Mama of planning something."

"But why would you think that?" Amelia demanded, giving him her full attention.

"She wants an interview with me tomorrow morning," Randolph replied. "Usually if she has anything serious to say to me, she communicates through you. Have you any idea what is in her mind?"

There was no time to tell him about what had transpired between her and her mother earlier today and Amelia regretted that she had not thought to have done it before. Still, there would be time enough for her to describe her victory to him later, if victory it really had been. She could not be certain yet. The idea of an interview between their mother and Randolph was somehow disturbing, although she was not quite certain why.

"Well then," Randolph proceeded, taking her silence as a negative reply, "there is one other thing. She is suddenly concerned about Grandfather's health. I heard her earlier this evening, and she was quizzing him about how he felt."

"I can imagine the sort of answer she received," Amelia replied. "Grandpapa does not care to think that he is mortal. But what do you think is going on?"

"Something," her brother replied ominously. "You can be assured that she has something up her sleeve. And if you find out what it is, you can oblige me by . . ."

But he was interrupted at that moment by someone calling out his name and they were joined by a pleasant-looking fellow in a yellow satin waistcoat who declared that he would like to be introduced, with which he bowed and ogled Amelia in what, no doubt, he took to be a vastly flattering manner.

"Amelia," Randolph said, "this is our hostess's son, the Viscount Featherstone himself, otherwise known as 'Pops.' My sister, sir."

"You cannot fool me, you gudgeon!" the viscount exclaimed. "I saw your sister only a moment ago on the other side of the room, talking to Witherspoon."

"That is my other sister, you muckworm you!" Randolph exclaimed. "I do have two, you know."

The viscount looked disconcerted. "Yes, yes, I know," he said. "But I was under the distinct impression that . . . Well, never mind! Better luck for me! She will not want to dance with you, now will she? My dear Miss Didright, may I claim you for the first cotillion?"

With a nod to her brother, Amelia took the young viscount's arm and allowed him to lead her to where the cotillion line was being formed. She saw Elizabeth close to the musicians, herself on the arm of a good-looking dandy and, remembered what Randolph had said about her sister going off in search of Darrow. Clearly she had not found him. Amelia was aware of a sense of relief.

"You may well be wondering why I did not believe that you could be Randolph's sister," her companion said as they stood waiting for the music to start. "Actually I have seen you before, in the company of your mother, but you look quite different tonight. And then there was what I heard my mother say when she was making out her list of guests for this affair."

"And what was that, sir?" Amelia said.

"No doubt I ought not to repeat it."

"Now I must insist that you tell me!" Amelia replied, plying her fan.

"She said that clearly you did not intend to marry and behaved yourself accordingly."

"How amusing!" Amelia said, although she found it anything but. "Is there more?"

"She said she found it quite incredible that anyone so beautiful should have decided to be a spinster," Lord Featherstone went on in his open way. "And then she added that you were like your mother in that you disapproved of Society and only went out in it to see your younger sister launched."

"I declare," Amelia said with a smile it cost her something to assume, "you must promise me to tell your mother that she is mistaken! There! The orchestra is about to play at last."

Throughout the dance, Amelia kept that same smile on her lips, but inside she was seething. Was it possible that she had presented such an image as Lady Featherstone had described? Last year, of course, she had been presented and returned to the country with such deliberate speed that no one had had the chance to come to know her. And this spring in all the flurry of seeing to the details of Elizabeth's coming-out, not to mention watching over her like a guardian angel, it was no wonder that she must have seemed to others to deliberately hover in the background. But it had never occurred to her that people had assigned a certain identity to her and that a reputation, once established, would stick. Lord Darrow was a case in point, although why his name came to mind she did not know. Once called a dandy, no doubt it was difficult to be thought of as anything else.

"Is something troubling you, Miss Didright?" Lord Featherstone inquired as the dance came to an end. "I hope it was not anything I said."

Assuring him that it was not, Amelia looked about the room and met the dark eyes of Lord Darrow who was standing alone in a corner. Amelia caught her breath, perhaps because she had not thought to see him. She had not quite remembered the chiseled, classic quality of his features. Tonight his skin seemed darker than before, no doubt because his fair hair had been powdered.

Unlike the evening before, when he had been dressed casually in riding costume, he was dressed all in black except for his flowing cravat, making a striking contrast with the other gentlemen in the room who were wearing the more conventional pastel colors favored by Society for evening dress.

She tore her eyes away from him, but not before she was aware of some unspoken message which had passed between them, the words of which she did not know. At the same time she became aware that the young viscount beside her was attempting to get her attention.

"I asked you if you would like some punch," he said when she had asked him to repeat what he had said. "Will you not allow me to fetch you some, Miss Didright?"

Amelia did not want the punch, but, flurried, she agreed to take a cup. As soon as the young gentleman had left her, Lord Darrow started across the floor. Although she did not look directly at him, she could see him well enough. And when her sister accosted him, Amelia made no pretense of not watching. She saw Elizabeth place one hand on his arm. She saw her tilt her head back and laugh at something the marquess had said. Elizabeth was at her most golden headed, charming best tonight, a lovely figure in a gown of primrose silk and no doubt Lord Darrow would be distracted. If only Lord Featherstone would return from the crowd about the punch bowl in the other room . . . Turning to look in that direction, Amelia was no longer forced to observe her sis-

ter's conquest. Her back was still to the scene
when she heard Lord Darrow's laugh and found
him, alone, beside her.

"In France they are particularly fond of the
gavotte," he said unexpectedly, with no prelude of
any sort. "Indeed, when I was in Paris two weeks
ago, it was being danced everywhere. Tell me,
Miss Didright, are you fonder of the gavotte than
of a cotillion?"

"What an extraordinary question to ask out of
the blue," Amelia replied.

"Ah, you are forthright as usual," Lord Darrow
replied. "That, at least, has not made a sudden
change. I am relieved to find it so."

"Why should you think there should be any
change?" Amelia retorted. "After all, not twenty-
four hours have passed since you saw me last, sir."

"I declare, Miss Didright, that it seems more."

He seemed to say it half in earnest, half in jest.
The bantering manner that he often assumed
made it difficult to know just how much of what
was said was meant. And yet Amelia realized that
it was as easy for her to talk to him as anyone she
had ever met. She wished she did not feel so guilty
at having used him, in a sense, to serve her
purpose, and took comfort in the thought that he
would never know of it.

"You have avoided the question, sir," she replied. "Why should there have been a change?"

"A change, Miss Didright! I would prefer to call
it a transformation. Last night at Vauxhall, you
were the very image of decorum. This evening

there is not a lady in the room more in the style of things."

"There is a certain consistency in our conversations, sir," Amelia said, "whatever change there may be in my appearance. Last night you criticized me for being frank one moment and arch the next; and this evening you remark on a difference of dress. I am not accustomed to being analyzed in such a fashion."

"Pray accept my heartfelt apologies for having been impertinent," Lord Darrow said. "If you will continue to be my mentor, no doubt I can become a better man."

Amelia could not resist laughing. It was all too absurd. The young marquess laughed with her and neither of them noticed Elizabeth watching from behind a column with her pretty face screwed up with rage.

Chapter 7

"**Really, Mama, I do not know how you can** sit in the card room and play whist, when Amelia is making a fool of herself in front of everybody!" Elizabeth said.

"From what you tell me, my dear, she has done nothing more than find his company amusing and be his partner in a gavotte," Lady Didright replied. "I will admit that is a dance which I think too vigorous to be quite proper, but I know I am old-fashioned."

They were standing in the changing room just off the blue salon where pins and mirrors and other such necessities as ladies might need had been provided by their hostess.

"In fact, my dear," Lady Didright continued, "when I looked out the whist room door not half an hour ago, I saw you prancing about on the dance floor in a manner I am certain that you know I do not approve of. However, we will let it pass. We will let everything pass for tonight. But I must warn you, my dear. Tomorrow there will be a change."

And, with that ominous rejoinder, she left her younger daughter to stare after her.

"I do not know what has come over Mama," Elizabeth told her brother with a worried frown a few minutes later, for she thought it in both their interests to share news of any shift in parental behavior. Over the years both she and Randolph had become skilled in ignoring their mother's complaints, knowing that she would never scold them long but turn instead to Amelia for enforcement.

"Everything is going wrong," Elizabeth continued. "Mama acts so strange and Amelia, too. Only see her now, laughing with Lord Darrow as though she did not have a care in the world!"

"Perhaps tonight she does not feel she has," Randolph replied. Together with Hanger, who had made an unexpected appearance with his sister, he had been helping himself liberally to the port wine and had reached a euphoric state in which nothing could bother him unduly, not even his mother's odd behavior. Besides, he was fond of Amelia and had long since felt that she should be allowed a better time.

"I cannot think what Lord Darrow sees in her," his sister grumbled.

"Then you have not looked very closely," Randolph replied. "Dash it if she's not as handsome as any lady in the room tonight and just as fashionable. It is only sour grapes on your part, Beth, if you think any differently."

Since this was not at all what his sister wished to hear, she changed the subject with alacrity. "Lord Berkeley *will* hang about me so," she muttered angrily. "He frightens everyone else away. I imagine that is the reason Lord Darrow has not asked me to take the floor. No doubt he does not want to undercut his friend."

"Randolph, you old rapscallion you!" the Honorable George Hanger announced, appearing out of nowhere with a flush on his face which rivaled the pink of his embroidered satin frockcoat. "Featherstone here has a fine plan to put a bit of spice in the evening; and we want you with us."

"Oh yes!" the Honorable Lucy Hanger cried, emerging from the crowd in company with their hostess's son who was as deeply in his cups as was possible for someone who could still stand on two feet, albeit not too steadily. "Such an exciting plan! There is to be a phaeton race around the square!"

"Dashed good idea!" Lord Featherstone observed, draping himself about the Honorable George Hanger for support. "Bit of sport. Just what the doctor ordered."

Randolph had the wit to hesitate but only for a moment. After all, what harm could it do? A fellow must be allowed a prank or two and this counted for nothing when compared with some of the stunts his grandfather had been up to forty years ago. Besides, the wine had given him a certain glow that needed to shine somewhere, and why not at the reins of a horse being driven full out around Grosvenor Square?

"It's on!" he cried and saw the excitement in his sister's eyes mirrored in those of the Honorable Lucy Hanger. It struck him that there were worse things than impressing that young lady. Dash it, he would cut himself a figure. See if he would not!

Plans were made accordingly. The Honorable George Hanger had his own phaeton just outside and Featherstone's was easily available. When Randolph admitted that he and his family had arrived in a curricle, his host suggested that a third phaeton be borrowed from another guest.

"No need to ask permission," he declared. "All for one and one for all," which dubious philosophy was echoed by the group as being eminently reasonable.

"Darrow will make a fourth!" the Honorable George Hanger declared. "He came alone in his own phaeton so that is easy enough. Can't do without Darrow, can we, lads?"

There was a general agreement that it would be most unfair to deprive a friend of such an opportunity. Elizabeth was loud in her enthusiastic support of the idea.

"The trouble is, he's bound to win," Randolph observed, but in the general clamor this observation went unheard except by Elizabeth who threw her brother such a threatening glance that he did not repeat himself. Hanger was duly sent off to make the proposition and was subsequently observed interrupting Lord Darrow in an animated, conversation with Amelia. Elizabeth drew her breath in between her teeth when the Honorable George returned to the group unaccompanied, with Lord Darrow and her sister taking their position on the dance floor for the next gavotte.

"Don't know what's got into the fellow," Hanger grumbled as he rejoined them. " 'Pon my soul, he wouldn't even listen to the proposition. Just said he was engaged to the lady for the next dance. We have your sister to thank for that, Didright old man."

"How like Amelia to put a damper on things," Elizabeth grumbled. "No doubt Lord Darrow will not be pleased a whit when he discovers the fun he's missed."

The other guests were too intent on their own affairs to notice the five young people leave the ballroom and the house. The night was mild and the two ladies did not bother with their wraps. Grosvenor Square lay sleepily under the gentle touch of moonlight, the road embracing it lined with carriages of various varieties, tended by an occasional driver. For the most part, however, the liveried servants who had conveyed their masters and mistresses here, were gathered underneath one of the brightly lighted windows engaging in a game which involved the tossing of dice.

"We'll be off and away before we draw any notice," the Honorable George Hanger muttered as they paused on the top step just outside the door.

"What about the footmen who saw us out?" Randolph demanded.

"Damme, their job's to stand beside the blasted door," Featherstone replied. "No business of theirs if I want to go outside. What's the matter with you, Didright? Think one of them's going to run to tell my mother, do you? You're a sapskull. No doubt about it."

The wine he had consumed, it seemed, had inflamed his temper and it was only with an effort that Hanger kept Featherstone from going at Randolph with his fists.

"I doubt that you can hold the reins, let alone drive a carriage," Randolph muttered.

"Fifty guineas will see you wrong!" Lord Featherstone replied. "I can hold my claret with the best of them, you jackanapes!"

Elizabeth saw her brother take a step backward. It was difficult to put Randolph in a temper, but she thought that Featherstone might well have just succeeded. Under ordinary circumstances she would never believe that Randolph would make a bet as high as the one suggested, but Featherstone had made this into a question of honor with his drunken ravings and calling of names. She felt a glow of pride when Randolph replied that he found the wager quite agreeable if Hanger agreed.

The Honorable George who was never short of funds said that he would be pleased to throw his hat in the ring, in a manner of speaking. A brief conference followed at which it was decided that the first gentleman to pass the steps on which they were standing for the third time around the square would be proclaimed the winner. Elizabeth and the Honorable Lucy Hanger were to act as judges in the event that the race should be close. Elizabeth's lace handkerchief was to become the flag which would be lowered at the start and finish and the Honorable Lucy Hanger was to give the starting command.

As it happened, they had been overly optimistic about the possibility of not attracting any attention. Even in the middle of the day it might have caused a mild sensation to see three young gentlemen, one of them clearly in his cups, lining three phaetons up across a road not wide enough to make it anything but a very thin squeeze indeed. The drivers were soon diverted from their dice and one of them came to the curb protesting that Randolph was in his master's carriage.

" 'E'll 'ave me 'ead if anything 'appens to it, sir," he pleaded.

It was at that point that Randolph had sufficient second thoughts to make him suggest to Hanger that all of this might not be a good idea.

"Afraid you'll lose your fifty guineas, are you!" Featherstone taunted him from his high seat. "Didright, you *are* a cub!"

Meanwhile the Honorable George Hanger had managed to calm the distressed driver and enlist the full encouragement of the others by promising to have a quantity of ale sent round from the nearest public house if the race could proceed without fear of interruption, whereupon such a considerable enthusiasm was generated that they would surely have been heard inside the house had it not been that the orchestra was playing at full tilt.

Thus it was that, with the grand house in the background and the street lined with cheering drivers, the Honorable Lucy Hanger cried out "Go!" Elizabeth lowered her handkerchief and the race began. The first lap was taken by Hanger who crouched on the leather seat and gripped the reins with such intensity that he might have been prodding his horse on through sheer will alone. "Go it, sir!" and like remarks greeted his passing but there was encouragement offered to Randolph, as well, and a general groan as Featherstone celebrated his first circling of the square by losing his grip on the reins completely and contenting himself with striking his bay smartly on the rump at regular intervals. Neither did it seem to trouble him unduly when his horse decided she might fare better if she came to a full halt, for when she did, the young gentleman appeared to fall into a sleep so deep that the shouting of the crowd did not waken him.

It was left to the Honorable George Hanger and Randolph to carry on. The second lap found Randolph in the lead, due to the fact that his borrowed phaeton took the corners more neatly than that of his friend. But the horse was skittish under an unfamiliar hand, and the third lap had only just started when Randolph realized that he had lost control of the animal altogether. Bucking and plunging, the frightened horse sought to free himself from the shaft. The noise was sufficient now to attract the attention of the guests inside the house and every window was crowded with onlookers.

And, indeed, the setting was very like a stage, thanks to the brilliance of the moonlight coupled with the drama of the events. The Honorable George Hanger had crossed the finish line and was being congratulated by his sister who was jumping up and down. Elizabeth, on the contrary, was screaming that someone must save her brother. Randolph was clutching the rails of the high phaeton seat with one hand and attempting to use the reins with the other to make the horse settle. In his own carriage, Lord Featherstone slept on, oblivious to the excitement. The drivers formed a liveried Greek chorus of suggestion, none of which was followed.

Just when it appeared that the frightened horse was determined to buck until the carriage had been reduced to splinters and Randolph thrown to the ground, a gentleman could be seen running toward the scene of the incipient tragedy. At the risk of being trampled, he caught the horse's harness by the bridle and skillfully began to quiet the creature.

"You had better get down, Didright," Lord Darrow said when the horse was doing nothing more than raising its hooves a few inches from the ground in a nervous, in-place trot. "It's bad luck but it's my guess you have a bit of explaining to do. I shouldn't like to be in your shoes."

Chapter 8

The moment she had heard the uproar out-side over the sound of the music, Amelia had somehow been quite certain that Randolph was involved. Flying to one of the long windows which faced the square, with the young marquess behind her, she had taken one look at the scene and whispered her brother's name. Only when Lord Darrow had left her, calling back a hasty assurance, did she notice that her sister was involved as well. In clear sight of everyone in the house, Elizabeth was jumping up and down in the street, waving a white handkerchief and screaming.

Amelia saw every detail of the rescue and only when it was completed did she give a thought to her mother. If Lady Didright had seen what was happening, Amelia knew that she would be in a sorry state indeed. Her hope was that, the whist room being toward the back of the house, her mother had not been able to gain an observation space. Still, someone was certain to tell her what had happened soon enough. To prevent that eventuality, Amelia began to search the room, and soon discovered the little sparrow of a woman vainly asking those taller than herself what was going on outside.

There was nothing for Amelia to do but to tell the truth. Her first impulse was to get her mother home as soon as possible under some pretext or other and then decide precisely what she would say. Surely there must be some way of not putting it badly. To simply announce that Randolph had been racing two other gentlemen about the square in a borrowed phaeton and that Elizabeth had been cheering him on would surely guarantee hysteria. As a consequence she spoke of a "boyish prank," and stressed the fact that the hostess's son was also involved, not going quite so far as to add that Lord Featherstone was presently sleeping off an excess of claret in the open air.

"But I'm sure I don't understand," Lady Didright kept repeating in a frantic manner. "How could Randolph do such a silly thing? I'm sure it is the company he keeps! Oh dear! Oh dear! Whatever shall I do?"

It was only natural, Amelia thought, that she should feel very guilty indeed. In the ordinary way of things this never would have happened since she would have been close enough to Randolph and Elizabeth to overhear their plans and put a stop to any foolishness at once. Now, although her mother had the goodness not to blame her, Amelia wondered if she had not been very selfish indeed. She *had* been frivolous, enjoying the attentions Lord Darrow had lavished on her at the expense of her responsibilities. Truth to tell, she had not given a thought to either her brother or her sister for the entire evening. And now see where that had brought them!

Lady Didright was mopping at her eyes when Lord Darrow appeared with Elizabeth in tow. "I think she should be taken home at once," he murmured to Amelia, "since she is clearly in an overexcited state. Randolph wants you to know that he will remain behind in order to make apologies to the owner of the phaeton he was driving. He wishes to apologize to his hostess, as well, for the disturbance he helped create. After that I will take him home."

Amelia thought that he was right about Elizabeth. Her sister's cheeks were stained with tears shed in her anxiety and her arms clutched Lord Darrow's so tightly that it was only with an effort that he was able to disengage himself.

"Mama," Amelia said. "I would like to introduce you to Lord Darrow."

Lady Didright started at the sound of the marquess's name and then, before Amelia could do anything to prevent it, her mother was haranguing him. She might have known, she said, that he was responsible for leading dear Randolph astray. Oh, yes, she had heard of him, she said, and she knew he was a rogue. In her excitement she lost all control, and there would have been no accounting for what she might have gone on to say if Amelia had not led her away with Elizabeth tagging reluctantly behind.

"You should have thanked him!" Amelia declared when they were finally in their carriage and being driven away. "He saved Randolph from a dreadful accident."

But this Lady Didright firmly refused to believe. She would not hear Lord Darrow's name mentioned again in her presence, she said in a shrill voice and with marked determination. Then she proposed that she was about to faint and Amelia was occupied for the remainder of the journey in applying a vinaigrette and lightly tapping her mother's cheeks to restore circulation. When they were inside the house and Lady Didright had been put in the care of her maid, she breathed a sigh of relief, only to discover that now she must turn her attention to Elizabeth.

"I suppose you can hardly wait to tell her about me," her sister declared angrily. "No doubt you will say that I encouraged Randolph when actually nothing could be further from the truth. Actually all of this is your fault for if you had not been making eyes at Lord Darrow he would have listened to what his friends were proposing and have nipped the idea in the bud."

They had returned to the blue salon which had two windows on the street from which Amelia intended to watch for her brother's return. Shaken as she had been by the recent turn of events, Amelia wanted nothing more than to be left alone.

"I do not intend to quarrel with you," she told her sister wearily. "You would be sensible to go to bed. As for telling Mama that you were out there on the street, I will leave that for you to decide, although I warn you that you were observed by so many people that she is quite certain to hear of it."

Elizabeth's golden curls were tangled and her primrose gown was nowhere near as dainty as it had been when she had left the house. In the ordinary way of things, Amelia would have seen her upstairs herself, but tonight she found she had no patience for such an undertaking.

"I will tell her that I was trying to prevent Randolph from making a fool of himself," Elizabeth said, stamping her feet. "No, I will tell her the truth!"

"Which is?"

"That Mr. Hanger challenged him in a way which Randolph could not refuse and still maintain his honor."

"Honor," Amelia said. "That is a strange word to use in this connection."

"Oh, *you* would not understand!" her sister pouted. "When one gentleman challenges another to a wager, only a cad would dare refuse."

Amelia frowned. "A wager?"

"Fifty guineas!" Elizabeth declared and then, realizing that she had said more than she intended, she pressed one hand to her lips.

"Oh dear," Amelia replied. "He will have to go to Mama for it."

Elizabeth's blue eyes grew very cold and hard. "You could make her understand that it was all— all a mistake," she said. "Yes, Amelia, you could read both Randolph and me a scold as you used to do, and then go to Mama and make it right."

Suddenly Amelia saw very clearly that she had been far more responsible for her brother's and sister's irresponsible ways than she had realized. Elizabeth had put it in a nutshell without exactly realizing the significance of what she said. She and Randolph had allowed her to berate them, even promised to mend their ways and, at times, actually done so, in return for which she had made their offenses seem slighter to their mother. Thus, in the interests of keeping the household peace, Amelia saw that she had contributed to her brother's recklessness and Elizabeth's selfish character.

"The time has come for you and Randolph to deal directly with Mama," she said in as gentle a voice as she could manage. "It was never wise of me to be a go-between. I realize that at last."

Elizabeth stamped her feet again. "The only thing you realize is that you do not wish to be troubled with us," she declared angrily. "Now that you have fallen head over heels in love with . . ."

"*That* is quite enough!" Amelia said with such a remarkable degree of firmness that Elizabeth was silenced. "I will not listen to such folly. I am in love with no one! But I will amuse myself as I please, and nothing you can say will stop me. And now perhaps you will do me the goodness of leaving me alone. I intend to wait up for Randolph to see that he is safely home."

For a moment she was afraid that her sister might have overheard what Lord Darrow had murmured to her about bringing her brother back to Portman Square, but apparently Elizabeth neither knew nor cared how Randolph was to return, for she stormed out of the room and up the stairs. Amelia followed her as far as the hall to tell the footman that he was no longer needed for the night.

"When my brother returns, I will let him in myself," she said and returned, with languid steps, to the salon. Elizabeth's outburst had quite disheartened her. If it was true that she was so much responsible for the way her brother and sister behaved, did it not follow that she should continue to be watchful, at least, and to advise them? And yet she knew that she could no longer mold her life that way. In the end it would be fair to no one. Her mother must be allowed to deal with her responsibilities in the best way that she could. Amelia must have her own life and Elizabeth and Randolph must accept the penalties for their own mistakes.

There was only a single candle burning in the blue salon, spattering shadows on the floor. When Amelia saw someone standing beside the Chippendale armchair in the corner, she gave a little cry. Only then did she see that it was her grandfather, still in his old-fashioned dressing gown, cradling the now empty bottle of claret in his arms.

"Sorry if I startled you, gel," he said in his rusty voice. "The fact is, I seem to have fallen asleep here in this chair. Did a bit of eavesdropping when I woke up and heard you and your sister talking. Bit of a rumpus at Lady Featherstone's, eh? Does my heart good to hear it."

There was nothing for Amelia to do but sketch in the details for him and watch his grin grow so broad it threatened to split his wrinkled face in two.

"Just like your mother to place the blame all wrong," he said when she had finished. "Damme if young Darrow doesn't sound like a pretty fellow! I fancy you'll take up the cudgels in his defense tomorrow."

"I intend to say nothing more on the subject," Amelia told him. "It would do no good, at any rate. Mama is convinced he is a scoundrel. Your recommendation of him this morning seems to have had a striking effect. Besides, I cannot think that he could care anything for her opinion, particularly after what she said to him tonight."

Lord Wellingham let one eyelid droop in a slow and excessively meaningful wink. "Dash it, my dear, he'll need her approval if he intends to offer for you."

"The gentleman and I scarcely know one another, Grandpapa," she protested. "There is no question of his making me an offer, I assure you."

"Demure as a nun's hen, ain't you?" the old man replied in the most exasperating way.

"You must be very tired, Grandpapa," Amelia said dryly. "Indeed, I urge you to go to bed."

"Eh, gel! What would you say if I told you I would prefer to talk about the condition of your heart?"

"I would say," Amelia replied tartly, "that I intend to say nothing. If you remain with me, you must be content to put up with my silence."

And, with that, she shut her mouth very tightly indeed and, shaking with silent laughter, Lord Wellingham shuffled toward the door. What she had said or done to so amuse him was beyond Amelia but she did not trouble herself over it. With bated breath she waited for him to leave her in peace. But, at the door, the old man turned.

"I'll just wait out in the hall," he told her. "That way I'll be the first to see young Randolph when he comes in."

Not for the first time, Amelia wondered if her grandfather made an irritation of himself deliberately or whether it was done all unsuspecting on his part. At all events, how cleverly he had made her break her vow of silence!

"Please don't do that," she pleaded. "There is no need. I've told the story. Nothing will be accomplished by having it told over again. If it is details you are after, tomorrow will be soon enough."

"Soon enough for you, gel, but not for me," his Lordship told her. "When you're my age, you'll realize that if you want something the night before it's just as well not to put off the getting to the next day."

Having failed with one, Amelia took another argument. "You will not be doing Randolph a favor, Grandpapa, if you show that you admire him for what he has done. Consider the facts. He took another gentleman's carriage. He nearly destroyed that carriage. And he risked his own life. Add to that the fact that he made a disastrous wager . . ."

"Ah, well, as for the wager, I heard Elizabeth mention that. Fifty guineas, eh? That's a true gentleman's amount."

"You see," Amelia said hopelessly. "You mean to tell him that, no doubt. Instead of which he should be brought to see what folly he has committed."

The old man hobbled back toward her, one finger beside his nose. "Mind you, his mother will see to that," he said. "Or put you to work for her. That's the more likely thing."

"If she wishes to rebuke either Elizabeth or Randolph in future, Mama must do so herself," Amelia replied.

"Fine new aims, eh?" her grandfather remarked. "Ah, well. I hope you keep to them, gel. Kiss your old grandfather good night and he'll be off to bed. Mind you tell my grandson I'm expecting to hear all about it tomorrow. Queensberry is certain to have heard of it, you see, and it would be a sorry thing if the lad's own grandfather didn't know the details."

He continued his muttered monologue as he took his departure and Amelia could not help but smile. Exasperating as he was, there was something about the old man which made for a special fondness in her heart. She wished her mother could appreciate him better and, at the same moment, it came to her that if she were no longer to stand between her mother and Elizabeth and Randolph, she would likewise not stand as buffer between her grandfather and his daughter.

But this was soon forgotten when she heard the sound of a carriage coming along the silent street. Taking up the candle, she went to peer out the window, pushing back the scarlet, velvet drapes to do so. The moon was no longer so bright and she was forced to lean close to the glass in order to see anything.

The phaeton was at the curb before she could make it out. Lord Darrow was driving, with Randolph beside him. When the horses came to a stop, Randolph did not get down immediately and, while he and Lord Darrow talked, the marquess was turned away from the house. But when, quite suddenly, Randolph swung himself to the ground, Lord Darrow turned about in the seat and looked directly at her.

In her eagerness to see her brother safely home, Amelia had forgotten how well the candle would illuminate her face, how clearly she could be seen from the outside. Before she could move away from the window, Lord Darrow had drawn off his three-cornered hat and swept it before him in a bow. For a long moment his eyes held hers. The noise Randolph was making at the door was just sufficient to break the spell and Amelia turned away from the window. When she had reached the hall and was reaching for the chain, she heard the sound of wheels and felt a stabbing of regret that they should be taking him away again.

Chapter 9

"There'll never be a better time to put your plan into effect," the duchess said. "I thought of that the very instant that I heard what happened at Lady Featherstone's last night. That is why I came to you at once. Is it true your son wagered fifty guineas? I assure you, my dear Selina, that if that is indeed the case, you must draw the pursestrings shut at once!"

Lady Didright let her head, encased this morning in a large mopcap, fall back against the cushions of the *causeuse* which filled the alcove of the window of her boudoir. As she had explained to her friend when she had been ushered upstairs, she was much too exhausted to think of facing her family this morning. It had been on that occasion that the duchess had suggested that this was no time to delay an introduction of the new order of things.

"Nothing could be more to your advantage than that they must all be feeling guilty now," her Ladyship continued as she paced restlessly up and down the little room, filling it with her turban and her feathers and her billowing skirts. "Randolph has made an utter fool of himself and Elizabeth has done very little better indeed. They tell me that she and the Honorable Lucy Hanger were actually cheering their brothers on! And, as for Amelia, she must realize that if she had not been so busy enjoying herself with Lord Darrow, she might have prevented this catastrophe."

Lady Didright sighed very deeply. She might have known she could have expected no comfort from dear Dorelle. A marvelous person, of course, but *so* forthright. Lady Didright closed her eyes and wished that she could remain forever in the safety of her private apartments.

"Besides," the Duchess of Bradlaw went on, "it will do you no good to linger about up here in your dressing gown. Your abigail's name is Mary, isn't it? Mary! Mary! Your mistress wishes to be dressed."

Mary had been Lady Didright's abigail for many years and, as she came into the little room, it was very clear that she did not relish being ordered about by someone else, even if that person had an important handle to her name.

"You take my word, ma'am, and you'll go back to bed," this personage announced, fixing her small eyes on her mistress sternly. "By the look of the sheets, you did nothing but toss and turn all night and as for the black shadows under your eyes . . ."

"The duchess is quite right, Mary," Lady Didright intervened. "I must get dressed. I do not care what gown. Lay out what you wish."

"It is indeed high time you changed your ways," the duchess muttered when Mary had left the room, her shoulders arched in disapproval. "Why, even your servants treat you casually. You *must* take a stronger line, Selina! I can do nothing to help you if you will not, at least, make the effort."

"Yes, yes, I know," Lady Didright replied distractedly. "But you must realize, my dear Dorelle, that it is not quite as simple as you make it sound."

The Duchess of Bradlaw puffed out her cheeks in the manner of one who faces a listless student who must, quite literally, be led everywhere by the hand. "Your first step is simplicity itself," she said. "You will see Randolph this morning and tell him that you absolutely refuse to give him fifty guineas unless he agrees to very strict conditions governing his future conduct."

Lady Didright propped herself up on one elbow and stared at her friend in consternation. "Fifty guineas!" she exclaimed. "Why on earth should I give him fifty guineas?"

"Because, my dear, if he is to be thought a man of honor, he must pay his debts," the duchess said patiently.

"Debts!" Lady Didright cried in a state of mounting excitement. "Debts! How can he suddenly have debts to that amount?"

"A wager may be counted as a debt, I think. A lost wager, to be exact."

"What wager? Do you mean to drive me mad?"

"I see that you know nothing about it," the duchess said with an air of satisfaction. "No doubt your children thought you had suffered enough shocks for one evening. The fact is, my dear Selina, that a certain Mr. Hanger, second son of the Viscount Hanger, named the price. The winner of the race was to collect that sum from each of the other two participants. You *do* know that young Lord Featherstone was the third gentleman involved? Ah, well he was. You can imagine his mother's state of mind. I mean to see her later today to offer my condolences. Young Featherstone was so deep in his cups that he became unconscious. At least that is what they say. All London is talking of the event, you know. No one speaks of anything else."

Lady Didright dared to wish that the duchess had not come to visit her so early with such a quantity of good news. The fact that Randolph had wagered fifty guineas was enough to throw her into a fit of hysterics. But with Dorelle here she did not dare. Dorelle was determined that she should appear strong and, if she did not want her to withdraw her help entirely, she must make the effort.

"Now, this is what must be done," the duchess said when Lady Didright was dressed and had exchanged her mobcap for one of her squashed turbans. "You must go downstairs to the library. Yes, the library will do quite nicely. Setting is so important, I think. And when you have settled yourself behind the desk, you must have your son brought to you."

Lady Didright nodded her head. So far nothing had been suggested which would seem to strain her capacity. What followed would provide the difficulty. Randolph had never paid her any heed before and she could not bring herself to believe that he would do so now, no matter what the circumstances. Still, a young gentleman must have money, and . . .

"Are you attending to me, Selina?" the duchess said with a sharp edge to her voice. "Do try to keep your mind on what I am saying. When Randolph comes in to the room, ask him to sit down and then . . ."

"I will tell him that I know everything!" Lady Didright declared. "I will say that words cannot convey how very shocked . . ."

"You will do nothing of the sort!" the duchess said, throwing out her bosom in a menacing way. "That would be to give him the easy way out of it. He would be forced to watch you put on a scene with no demand that he participate. No, no! Instead you will ask him to give you the details of what occurred last night. Tell him it is useless to skip over anything, since someone is bound to come to you with the news. Be very calm. But icy. The last thing that you must do is show emotion."

"Oh, dear!" Lady Didright wailed. "That will be very difficult, I'm sure. Besides, Randolph is certain to know that something is wrong."

"And so he should," the duchess assured her.

"That is the first part of the punishment. He must be given an opportunity to feel some trepidation. To wonder what will come next. You have been far too predictable in the past. They know you will weep and wring your hands and that will be the end of it. This time let your son see from the start that there has been a change. Let his skin crawl a bit."

This last was said with such a degree of relish as to make Lady Didright wonder whether it might not be that her old friend took pleasure out of planning punishment that was greater than strictly customary.

"And then?" Lady Didright inquired in a small voice.

"Say nothing. Make no comment. Let him tell his story. And when he is finished, simply say, 'Surely there is more.' "

"But what if there is not?"

The duchess gave her an impatient look. "There is always more!" she said. "Make him tell the story over and request that he be detailed."

"And what if he refuses?" Lady Didright knew her son.

The duchess drew herself up as though she had been challenged personally. "He will *not* refuse," she said. "In the first case, he will be too much taken aback to find you behaving in an unaccustomed way. Secondly, if you are determined that he will tell you everything, then he will. If I could convince you of that one fact, my dear Selina, I would have settled everything. Other people recognize determination. And they respond to it."

"Oh, I do hope that you are right, Dorelle! But then—when everything is told. What do I say next?"

The duchess leaned against the mantelpiece. Because of her extreme height, it was not an awkward gesture. The morning sun which was pouring through the window made her bulging brown eyes glisten like soft molasses and added somehow to the commanding thrust of her nose.

"You tell him that you will not give him the fifty guineas until you have his promise to allow you to pass on his associates. That is to say, all decisions as to whom he will make his friends will be in your hands. Make it very clear there will be no exceptions. And, if he is not quick enough to realize what it will mean to his reputation if he does not pay Mr. Hanger immediately, you can remind him."

Lady Didright darted about her friend in a sudden, little flurry. "You make it all sound so very simple, my dear Dorelle!" she cried. "And I am sure that it is not!"

"One step at a time," her mentor replied. "The great thing is to keep your head. After your son has been dealt with, you can attend to your father. The old man must be kept out of Queensberry's way as much as possible, particularly after what has happened."

"Oh, dear, oh dear!" Lady Didright exclaimed. "So much to do."

"I will see you through, my dear," the duchess assured her. "If I can assist in settling your household problems, I will think of it as my greatest coup for I have rarely seen a family in such general disarray. We will confer about Elizabeth and Amelia tomorrow. I have a plan for how to deal with both of them quite satisfactorily."

Lady Didright paused in flight and gave a little shudder. "I hope it will all come right," she said. "Indeed I do. Because what will happen otherwise, I do not dare to guess. I feel, somehow, as though I were on the brink of a great catastrophe!"

Chapter 10

"When she threatened to withhold my own money from me, I could not believe my ears," Randolph said. "And when she proposed to choose my friends for me in future, I was quite certain that one of us had gone mad."

"But it appears she means what she says?" Amelia asked him. "Will she refuse to be swayed?"

They had been walking about the square for nearly an hour, discussing what had just occurred. Randolph had come directly from his interview with his mother in the library to seek his elder sister out.

"The most extraordinary thing has happened," he had told her, his face gone quite white. "I need to discuss it with you somewhere we will not be interrupted, or for that matter, overheard."

Amelia knew her brother well enough to recognize that he was seriously disturbed. She had spent a restless night, her mind turning the pages of the evening past over and over again until everything that had happened was firmly fixed in her mind. And always she came back to that moment when Lord Darrow had seen her in the window. Something stirred inside her each time she remembered the way their eyes had met. It was like stepping on a stair, only to find it is not there. A sudden lurch inside. A shifting. It was a feeling she had never had before. It troubled her so much that she had welcomed Randolph and his problem as a distraction.

Now she matched her walk to his and considered the situation. It was a mild May morning with the chestnut trees blooming with fresh, green leaves and daffodils nodding their fragile heads along the border of the path. Amelia had intended to go riding in the park and so she wore, as walking-out dress, her riding habit with a dark blue, double-breasted jacket and a full blue skirt. Her riding hat and cravat were mannish, as well, since it was the fashion, but Randolph thought he had never seen her look more beautiful with her blue eyes wide with concern and the breeze stirring her black curls about the perfect oval of her face.

"This is not like Mama," Amelia reflected aloud. "Which means that she is taking advice from someone. Yes, why did I not think of it before! The Duchess of Bradlaw was at the house this morning. I happened to see her being ushered into Mama's boudoir. For all we know, she might be there still. After all, she only lives across the square. She would not have arrived in her carriage."

"And everyone knows what a meddler she is," Randolph agreed. "That must be it. Mama has asked that woman to counsel her. That is strange enough in itself, dashed if it isn't! When she needs help in keeping any one of us in line, she makes a habit of going straight to you, Amelia. You know as well as I that that has always been her way before."

Amelia remembered that Randolph knew nothing directly of the fact that she had led their mother on to lose her trust in her. She thought of explaining to him now how she had used Lord Darrow's reputation—or, at least, her mother's perception of it—to tarnish her own. And then she hesitated. But, when her brother continued to fuss about the matter, she realized that she must tell him.

"No, I cannot go to Mama and settle anything," she told him. "It's too late for that."

And then she told him how it had all worked out thanks to the attentions Lord Darrow had shown her during the expedition to Vauxhall, their grandfather's subsequent recommendation of that gentleman to their mother and Elizabeth's biased report of her sister's behavior.

"And so she thinks you are no longer to be depended on!" Randolph explained. "It has all worked out the way you wanted it."

"But not to our mutual advantage, it seems," Amelia told him as they turned out through the iron gates of the square and wandered in the direction of Hyde Park. "It did not occur to me that she would turn to anyone else. And, although I must confess to wanting her to take the reins of our household into her own hands, I never in the world suspected that she would do so with such a vengeance."

Randolph tipped his tri-cornered hat to a gentleman passing, but Amelia allowed herself no such distraction. How like her brother to be faced with such a serious problem, and still be able to look for the familiar face in the crowd.

"Well, what do you intend to do?" she said impatiently. "You must give Mr. Hanger the fifty guineas. That is a large amount of money, Randolph. I do not think that you have any choice except to give in to her demands. Your inheritance will not be yours to do with as you like for another year."

"Perhaps Hanger will agree to wait that long," Randolph muttered. "Dash it, Amelia, how did I ever happen to do such a foolish thing?"

As usual she could not help but feel a twinge of sorrow for him. That was the way it had been in the past. Randolph was as quick to admit that he had made a mistake as he was to make it in the first place. She wondered if he had said much the same thing to their mother and, if he had, how that lady had been able to resist. They had all contributed to spoiling him, no doubt. If only their father were still alive . . ."

"It might be," Amelia said slowly, "that you would not be mistaken to take Mama's advice. I mean, the idea of the race was not yours, I expect."

"No, it was Hanger's," Randolph told her. "At least I think it was. To tell the truth there are peculiar gaps in my memory. Do you expect that I was in my cups?"

"I think it is quite possible," Amelia replied but not in a way as to rebuke him. That, at least, was to be a thing of the past. "You know the condition Lord Featherstone was found in. All of which strengthens the point I am trying to make. Mr. Hanger and Lord Featherstone and all the others who make up the Prince's group . . ."

"Including Lord Darrow."

"Yes, yes," Amelia said quickly. "I expect we must, although he was not at fault last evening. But the fact is that it might be just as well if you *were* to make other friends. I suspect that if you continue to make yourself a part of them, this is not the last bit of trouble you will find yourself in."

"No," Randolph said stubbornly, stepping to one side to allow a dray to pass. "I will choose my own friends. I am determined when it comes to that particular point, Amelia. They are decent fellows, all of them, and amusing to be with. These are the days I will remember best of all those of my life. At least that is what Grandfather says. You know as well as I what pleasure he takes in his own memories."

"I have heard all his stories a hundred times," Amelia replied. "Surely you do not admire such disgraceful behavior. It inspires no particular confidence in me to think that you have chosen Grandpapa for your model."

"I did not go so far as to say that," Randolph admitted. "I only mean I am determined to enjoy myself while I am still free to do so."

"And I will say again that I do not think you have any choice," Amelia said impatiently. "You must repay Mr. Hanger. Mama controls your inheritance for the time being. If you must change your company in order to get the money from her, then you must do so."

"Does it not occur to you that, if she succeeds in this, she may go on to interfere in the lives of everyone in the family?" Randolph protested.

There was more traffic now, both on foot and wheels and the park was still a distance away. Amelia wondered if they could not have chosen a better setting in which to talk, and was about to suggest that they return home when Randolph gave a shout.

"I have the answer!" he declared. "I will go to our grandfather for assistance. Whatever he gives me will be a loan, of course. I will repay him with interest if he likes as soon as I come into my inheritance."

Amelia turned to stare at her brother. Her old self would have disapproved but her new self considered Randolph's plan to be a distinct possibility. Her grandfather must have a fortune, surely. Her mother had complained to her more than once that, although it was not unreasonable to think that her father should contribute to his present upkeep, he had not given her a shilling since he had left his lonely estate in Yorkshire and come to live with them.

"I declare," she once had said, "sometimes I think Papa is perverse in everything. Mama often told me that money passed through his fingers like water when he was young, before they married. And now it seems that he has turned into a miser, at least as far as I am concerned. He knows I will not stoop to ask him for a single penny. Yes, no doubt that is the way of it. He would do anything to infuriate me."

Amelia wondered now if Randolph would find it as simple as he thought to be financed for a year by his grandfather. And yet she did not like to discourage him when he was so keen. In response to his whistle, a hackney cab had stopped beside them and the two young people boarded it with alacrity.

"Grandpapa will be with his friend Lord Queensberry at this hour of the morning," Randolph declared and directed the jarvey to Piccadilly, which crowded thoroughfare they reached directly, it not being a great distance from where their walk had taken them.

Lord Queensberry's bow window was not at all difficult to find since the house itself was distinguished by a peculiar structure on the street level, an enclosure into which his Lordship's carriage could be driven, allowing him to be placed inside it without public exposure.

"The fellow always had a spot of vanity," her grandfather had told Amelia once. "Now it has come down to a false eye and heaven knows what else to make him look alive. He takes care always to remain in his chair when company is present.

Damme, I suspect to watch him move is like observing a skeleton perambulate!"

"Just here!" Randolph shouted when they reached the spot and, handing the jarvey a coin or two, he helped Amelia to descend. The crowd of carts and carriages not to mention pedestrians was so thick at that particular point that it was quite ten minutes before brother and sister had reached the shelter of the doorstep. Looking up, they saw their grandfather, proudly installed beside his friend in the famous window, bowing and waving to passers-by of their acquaintance. It was a quaint scene which, in the ordinary way of things, would have given Amelia some amusement. Today, however, she could only muster a tentative smile when her grandfather noticed them.

The pantomime which followed caused a good many of those passing by to stare curiously at the young lady and gentleman standing on Lord Queensberry's doorstep, for Lord Wellingham expressed his delight by rapping on the window with his cane, while, in the chair beside him, Old Q bent down and squinted at them with what Amelia assumed must be his one good eye. A servant having, apparently, been dispatched immediately, they were soon being ushered into the presence of the two old gentlemen.

"Handsome pair, ain't they?" Lord Wellingham demanded, as though his two grandchildren were horses on show at Tattersall's. "Got a third at home to match them. But then, you know about Elizabeth."

"Eh?" Lord Queensberry inquired, placing a

splendid ear-trumpet to his ear. "What's that you say, Wellingham?"

"Better keep your voices high," their grandfather warned them. "Nothing makes Old Q fly into the boughs faster than not being able to hear what's being said."

And with that he repeated his previous comments in a loud and creaking treble.

But Lord Queensberry was not interested in Elizabeth. Both his real and his glass eye glistened as he turned his attention on Randolph.

"Hurly-burly thing you did last night, lad," he declared. "Put you in considerable ill odor, I suppose."

"My mother has cut off funds," Randolph shouted. "Unless I agree to allow her to choose my friends, I cannot even pay the wager I made with Hanger."

"Women!" Lord Queensberry declared expressively. "Never have them about if I can help it. Slipgibbets, every one of them."

"Stubble it!" was their grandfather's contribution. "Not let you have what's well and truly yours! I'll have a word with her, my boy. I won't allow her to cut your stick this way. She's still my daughter. I'll put her in mind of that!"

And before either Randolph or Amelia could stop him, he had hobbled out of the room, railing at one of the footmen to call him a carriage.

"Let him go!" Lord Queensberry shouted as the two young people showed some indication that they were about to follow their grandfather. "Thinks he's useless, poor chap. Complains of it to me. Damme if it won't do him the world of good to put the stand up to that daughter of his. Can't help it if she is your mother."

Amelia glanced at her brother and, between them, they came to a silent agreement. No doubt this strange, old man was right. After all, he had been their grandfather's friend for more than forty years. And so it was they spent an hour answering Lord Queensberry's questions about the affair of the night before. It was a revelation to see the way the old rogue went after bits and pieces of scandal, like a hungry hound nosing after scraps, Amelia thought. Perhaps that was what kept him so alert. As long as there was gossip, he was determined to thrive on it. No doubt his daily visits here to this bay-windowed room overlooking one of London's busiest streets helped keep her grandfather alive, as well. With this in mind she found she could not work up an irritation at his Lordship's curiosity and when, at last, she and Randolph rose to leave him, she bent and kissed the withered cheek much to the old man's delight.

"Keep out of mischief, gel!" he chortled. "And tell that grandfather of yours that I expect him here tomorrow."

Chapter 11

"I declare, my dear, you have done me proud!" the Duchess of Bradlaw told Lady Didright. "That is what comes of following my instructions to the letter, you see. How many times did you have him retell the story?"

"La, he looked at me so strangely when I asked him to go back and put in every detail," Lady Didright replied. "I did not want to tempt a rebellion by asking him to tell it to me a third time. But you were right, Dorelle. He was completely taken by surprise. Put on the defensive! Made to feel guilty! It made me think of all the opportunities I have missed to do the same thing in the past. But never mind. The fact is that he knows precisely where he stands. If he wants to keep his pride and pay the wager, he must change the company he keeps."

This morning, knowing that except for the servants they were alone in the house, the ladies had decided to confer in the blue salon. A tray of tea things was set on the low table between them and a low fire hissed in the hearth. Lady Didright wore the self-satisfied smile of one who has had her way and the duchess looked more than ever like a general who, having won one battle, is eager to go on to the next.

"I must tell you my plans for Elizabeth and Amelia," she said now. "But, before I do, you did not tell me whether or not Randolph agreed to your terms."

Lady Didright opened her gray eyes very wide. "Not in so many words, Dorelle," she replied. "But then he was so taken by surprise, I doubt he could have said a word. But I could tell by the way he left me that he realized there was no alternative to what I had proposed. I expect he will appear quite soon and ask for the fifty guineas. Oh dear! That is such a deal of money! I do wish it were less! But still—if he accepts my terms, I will have gained a good deal. I only hope that Amelia . . ."

"And what has Amelia to do with this?" the duchess thundered. "She was not present at the interview, I hope!"

"No, no!" Lady Didright protested. "I only meant to say that Randolph took her for a walk directly after he left me in the library. I saw them in the square and then they walked off toward the park. There was a time when I could have been certain that she would make him see that what I proposed was the only sensible way. But there has been such a change in the gel! I declare I do not know what to expect from her anymore."

The duchess seemed to expand like a balloon which has been suddenly inflated. "I do not think we need to concern ourselves with what Amelia has said or has not said," she declared stiffly. "There is no way out for Randolph. Do you think that if there had been I would not have seen it? I think we can accept the fact that that particular problem is solved. Now, let us consider Elizabeth."

"She is a very headstrong girl," Lady Didright admitted. "I do not think she will be as easy to deal with. She was actually out there on the street, you know, waving her brother on! She fancies doing the unusual."

"Yes, yes," the duchess said impatiently. "She is the sort who can ruin their reputation beyond repair in a single Season. Lady Hasting's daughter was the same, but I settled everything quite satisfactorily. Yes, I was very pleased with myself indeed, and Lady Hastings was delighted. I believe that the same tactic could be used in Elizabeth's case, with your kind approval."

"La! I am bound to approve of anything you recommend!" Lady Didright exclaimed.

The duchess smiled and settled herself more firmly in the chair. There was nothing she liked better than to be depended on. "Very well," she said. "You will see that I have only applied common sense to the situation. The aim in bringing any young gel to this city in the spring is to marry her. Am I correct?"

"But of course you are, my dear Dorelle."

"To marry her well. Titles and fortunes are an important consideration."

"Very important indeed."

"As important as the gel's happiness?"

"I would have thought one was dependent on the other."

The duchess laughed. "You are more of a cynic than I dared to hope, my dear Selina. What I am getting at is that it is easier to marry a gel to someone she fancies than otherwise. Young ladies are so likely to be romantic."

Lady Didright admitted that that was very true.

"Now, in the case of Lady Hasting's daughter, she fancied debauchees. I do not mean mere rogues, you understand."

"Dear me! Dear me!" Lady Didright cried, holding her cheeks in her hands.

" 'The main thing is to see her married before she spoils her reputation,' " I told her mother. " 'All that is necessary is that we find one of the type she likes who has a title and inheritance and point her in his direction.' "

The duchess gave a triumphant little laugh. "And that is what we did!" she concluded. "The gel was delighted to marry someone with such shocking habits and has, I believe, spent the five years since attempting to convince him to abandon them."

Lady Didright frowned. "I am afraid," she said, "I do not see . . ."

"Elizabeth is attracted to the sort of gentleman who makes up the Prince's group. Rakes, all of them. But only in their unmarried state. Let her have one of them. Speed is the essential thing. It must be accomplished before she disgraces herself which, I remind you, she nearly did the other evening at Dora Featherstone's."

"I suppose you could be right," Lady Didright began.

"Of course I'm right!" the duchess declared indignantly. "Who do you think she finds attractive? We will arrange an encounter. And then another. If they both are headstrong, we will not have to wait long. But we must have a name. Come! I have it! You told me before that she came to you a few days ago with a long complaint about Amelia's behavior with Lord Darrow at Vauxhall. Could that have been inspired by jealousy, do you suppose?"

"You do not think I would allow either of my daughters to marry Lord Darrow!" Lady Didright exclaimed. "Why, it was because of him . . ."

"It was because of him that your son did not crack his skull the other night," the duchess told her, clicking her fan against the arm of the chair. "I have had the story from others since I saw you earlier today, and they say that, if it had not been for the marquess, the carriage your son was riding in might very well have been overturned."

"I believe that you are asking me to be inconsistant!" Lady Didright cried, darting up from the chair in her excitement. "You know that it was because of Lord Darrow that I lost my confidence in Amelia. And yet I am supposed to find him the ideal suitor for her sister!"

The duchess expressed her exasperation by puffing out her cheeks in her accustomed way. *"Must* I explain everything to you, my dear Selina?" she demanded. "You wish to see Elizabeth married. Very well. Lord Darrow suits that purpose. With Amelia your aim is quite different. You wish to see her sensible again. Why, the two considerations complement one another! How better to convince her to become her old, commonsensical self than to disillusion her? And that will happen when we have arranged for Lord Darrow to offer for her sister."

Lady Didright was forced to admit that it was an admirable plan. If she had doubts, she was too wise to let the dauntless duchess hear of them. She was about to offer more elaborate congratulations, in order to give her friend what she clearly considered was her due, when the door to the blue salon burst open and her father appeared, a spectral form brandishing his cane at her.

"What's this I hear, gel?" he demanded, making an uncertain progress across the room, with no attention paid to the duchess who was eyeing him malevolently. "Damme, you can't cut the lad off from his funds! The devil will be to pay if you do!"

"My dear Lord Wellingham," the duchess declared, rising majestically from her chair. "How is it that no one has told me you have been ill?"

"Eh?" the old man exclaimed, taken off his guard. "Ill? Why, that's a tattlemonger's tale!"

"But surely you must have been," the duchess continued relentlessly. "Why, I have never seen you in so bad a color! Surely you must have been taken freakish."

"The only thing about me that is freakish," the

old man told her, "is my temper. And I'll admit to that willingly enough! Perhaps you will be good enough to leave me alone with my daughter."

"Papa," Lady Didright protested. "The duchess is my guest. You really cannot speak to her in that manner!"

"Dash it, I'll speak to her in any manner that I like," her father declared in a decided manner. "Meddling old muckworm! She put you up to it, I'll warrant!"

"Dear Lord Wellingham," the duchess said without a moment's hesitation. "You really must be seen by a physician. Selina! Surely you have noticed the blue tinge about your father's lips. And where his eyes should be white, they are quite yellow. When heart and liver are both affected, there should be no delay of treatment."

"Yellow!" the old man quavered. "Blue! I am not a rainbow, madam."

"I saw quite the same symptoms in Lord Rosemount just a week before he died," the duchess told him. And there is a twitch just on the right side of the nose which promises a nervous complaint."

Lord Wellingham was truly distracted by now, for he had always prided himself on his health and liked to compare it with that of Lord Queensberry to his advantage.

" 'Pon my soul, Selina," he said to his daughter. "Do you agree that I am looking poorly?"

Over his head, the duchess gave Lady Didright a look full of such intense meaning that she was thrown into a flurry.

"It may be, Papa . . ." she began.

"You will remember the physician I was speaking of the other day," the duchess interrupted. "Dr. Pinchpurse is his name. A brilliant man. Quite brilliant! With any number of new cures at his disposal."

"Oh yes! I *do* remember!" Lady Didright cried. "How clever of you to remind me, dear Dorelle! Indeed, Papa, I have been worrying about you. I did not like to speak of it for fear you would call me interfering."

"Interfering!" the duchess exclaimed. "Why, one has a responsibility to one's parents, my dear, particularly when they are getting on, and might be swept away in an instant by nothing more complicated than the common cold!"

"What is all this talk of death and dying!" Lord Wellingham protested. And yet it was clear that he was alarmed. His breath seemed to come in spurts and starts and the hand which held the cane began to shake as though he had the palsy. "Perhaps I do feel a bit faint. But it is nothing! Nothing! No doubt I came back from Piccadilly in too great a hurry."

"If you will take my advice, sir," the duchess said in a tone which indicated that he would be foolish if he did not, "you will permit me to send for Dr. Pinchpurse immediately. A stroke can come on in an instant, and as for heart attacks . . ."

She waved her hands as though, all about her, multitudes of people were about to draw their final breaths.

"I think that dear Dorelle is right, Papa," Lady

Didright said earnestly. "After all, it can do no harm. If nothing is wrong, there is only the fee to pay."

"The fee!" her father repeated, rousing for the moment at the thought of an expense.

"I will pay," his daughter assured him. "You know how much your well-being means to me. Come! I will call for your man to help you up to bed. And dear Dorelle will send a message off to Dr. Pinchpurse this very instant!"

Both of these tasks having been performed with considerable dispatch, the duchess turned to Lady Didright with congratulations. "I was afraid you had forgotten my plan," she said. "How nicely this has worked to our advantage. There was time for me to coach the dear doctor directly after I left you earlier this morning. The doctor knows the situation. By the time he has finished his examination, your father will be convinced that he should pay more attention to his health."

"Which means I will no longer have to worry about him making a public display with Lord Queensberry," Lady Didright declared with an air of great relief. "How clever you have been!"

"Yes, I believe I have," the duchess said in a self-satisfied manner. "I do believe that I have been very clever indeed."

Chapter 12

When Amelia and her brother returned to the house on Portman Square following their visit with Lord Queensberry, Elizabeth was waiting with the news.

"The doctor says that on no account is Grandpapa to leave the house except, perhaps, for a stroll about the square when the weather is fair," she said after she had recounted the circumstances which had brought a physician to the house. "There is damage to the heart and liver, it seems, and heaven knows how many other complaints."

Amelia broke her astonished silence. "But Grandpapa was in the best of health not quite two hours ago!" she exclaimed. "I cannot believe that he should have been brought to death's door in that short length of time."

To which response, Elizabeth declared that when

Amelia had seen him, she would change her mind. "It is fortunate that the duchess was here to spot the signs," she continued. "No doubt, as Mama says, it is only because we see him every day that we did not notice his decline."

"Nonsense!" Amelia replied. "I cannot believe it! Who is this Dr. Pinchpurse? What are his credentials?"

"He has the duchess to vouch for him," Elizabeth said stiffly. "Why, he has cured any number of her acquaintances."

The expression on Amelia's face revealed her opinion of the Duchess of Bradlaw more clearly than words could have ever done. Even Randolph could not prevent allowing a shadow of doubt to sweep across his face.

"Dash it, I have never trusted that particular lady," he muttered. "She takes too much upon herself, in my opinion. It is a pity that our own doctor is in the country. Why, we have never required one here in London. But I believe that we should have a second opinion."

Elizabeth arched her golden eyebrows. "Mama will not allow it," she declared. "It would be an insult to the duchess."

"I am not so much concerned with the duchess as I am for Grandpapa," Amelia said in a decided manner. "I quite agree with Randolph that we should have the opinion of another physician, and that immediately."

"Meddle! Meddle!" Elizabeth exclaimed. "That is all you ever do! No one is ever right except yourself! Very well. If you doubt my word that our grandfather is ailing, go upstairs and see for yourself."

Since this was what Amelia had intended, she lost no time in hurrying up the stairs with her brother close behind. The second door on the right was rapped on and opened, whereupon they found the old man propped up in his canopied bed with a tassled nightcap on his head and the tables on either side covered with bottles of medicine and packets of drugs of every sort. Lady Didright was darting around the room in her usual distracted fashion, while the duchess loomed beside the wardrobe. Beside the bed, facing the door, stood a thin man in black frock coat and pantaloons who was distinguished only by a crooked nose and the extraordinary length of his arms.

"Grandpapa!" Amelia cried. "How could all this have happened so suddenly?"

The old man turned slowly on his pillow. The ivory false teeth which he prided had been removed, throwing the bottom part of his face into great hollows. This alone was quite sufficient to make him appear to be in a decline, but there was also a languid air about him as though he had scarcely the energy to move his head. His answer to Amelia was a sigh.

"The patient cannot sustain a conversation in his present condition, I fear," the man in black said dolefully, looking down at Lord Wellingham with a tragic expression. "He must be kept as quiet as possible."

And, reaching out with one of his long arms, he

placed his hand on the old man's forehead as though to test for fever.

Amelia felt a flicker of real alarm. Either her grandfather was very ill or he had been made to believe himself to be and, at his age, either possibility was equally fraught with danger.

"This is Dr. Pinchpurse, my dears," Lady Didright announced. "We are so fortunate to have him. Indeed, he put off the Earl of Huntington to come to us."

"Perhaps you can tell me, Dr. Pinchpurse," Amelia declared, going closer to the bed, "precisely why you have seen necessary to remove my grandfather's false teeth. He cannot eat without them, you know."

The doctor's crooked nose twitched from side to side. "My dear young lady," he replied. "Your concern is admirable, but you must allow me to make all decisions. As for food, your grandfather's stomach cannot tolerate anything more than gruel."

"But only last night he ate a hearty meal of mutton, followed by the better part of an apple tart!"

She could not be certain but, for a moment, Amelia thought she saw her grandfather's eyes brighten.

"And tonight we are to have beef done just as you like it,' she went on. "And scalloped oysters, not to mention . . ."

"My dear Miss Didright!" the doctor protested, pressing the old man, who had begun to rise, down against his pillow. "I really must beg you not to excite your grandfather in this way."

"It would be better if you left him alone right now, Amelia!" Lady Didright exclaimed. "I know you want him well. As for that, we all do. But it will do no good to remind him of the sort of life he will never live again."

"You mean by that, I suppose," Amelia said defiantly, "that Grandpapa is never again to enjoy his bottle of claret."

The figure on the bed stirred restlessly under the doctor's hand.

"Never to sit with Lord Queensberry in the bow window facing Piccadilly in the morning sun watching the crowds stream by below and exchanging a few juicy bits of scandal."

At this her grandfather made what appeared to be a determined effort to sit bolt upright, but the doctor's arm was strong. Pressing the old man back against his pillows with one hand, he took his pulse with the other.

"I cannot insure that he is not seized by a fit of apoplexy if this goes on," he told Lady Didright. "Indeed I cannot!"

"Not a pleasant way to go to one's maker," the duchess was heard to observe to no one in particular. "But then, young gels care for nothing but their own convenience!"

Amelia stepped forward, her chin held high. "Perhaps you would like to explain what you mean by that, madam," she declared. "I assume you refer to me."

The duchess folded her hands just below her bosom and looked down her nose in a patronizing fashion. "I only meant that, no doubt, you feel it will put a crimp in the Season for you if there is a sick man in the house," she replied. "It does not suit you to have your grandfather ill, and so you try to persuade him otherwise. The doctor has just been telling us that, if Lord Wellingham returns to his old habits, he will be dead within a fortnight."

Amelia bit her lip and made no reply. On the one hand she had never liked the duchess. Certainly she did not trust her. And she was not impressed by Dr. Pinchpurse. But, if she was wrong, and her grandfather was truly in a dangerous condition, she was not behaving as she should in reminding him of past pleasures, encouraging him not to take the doctor's advice.

"It is my opinion, Mama," she said, turning her back on the duchess, "that we should call in another physician. I, myself, cannot believe Dr. Pinchpurse's diagnosis."

"Well, well, my dear," Lady Didright said. "We will talk about it in private. I think it best that you and Randolph leave the room. There is no reason for you to look so concerned. We only want what is best for your grandfather. You must believe that."

Amelia left, but not until she had pressed a warm kiss on the hollowed cheek. The old man's eyes were closed and she thought she smelt the acrid scent of laudanum on his breath, but she could not be sure.

"It will not do him any harm," Randolph protested when she told him her suspicions outside the bedchamber door. "It does him good to rest."

"So you mean to take sides with them!" Amelia

said sharply. She had thrown off her high-crowned riding hat when she had come into the house earlier, and now she ran the fingers of one hand through her tangled, black curls. Excitement had brought a high color to her cheeks and her eyes sparkled with anger. "Can't you see that they intend to convince him that he is an invalid?"

"But why would Mama do that?" Randolph demanded. "How would it be to her advantage? It seems a very cruel thing."

"She would not see it that way," Amelia said grimly. "Besides, she is clearly being influenced by that dreadful duchess. Indeed, that is where the real danger lies, in my opinion. Mama might be well pleased to find some way of keeping Grandpapa closer to this house. You know she thinks it hurts our reputation to have him make a public show of himself with Lord Queensberry. When we first came up to London, you will remember the fuss she made to keep him home. And now she has found a way to keep him off the streets."

"But to confine him to his bed ..." Randolph began. "Surely she would not go as far as that."

"*She* would not," Amelia declared. "I cannot tell what the duchess would or would not do. If you want my guess, I think Mama only hopes to make him so careful of his health that he will not wander far afield. But she allows herself to be influenced so. She is so weak in some ways and so determined in others."

They had started toward the winding stairs which led down to the hall but now Randolph paused. "Is it possible do you think," he said in a low voice, "that the duchess advised Mama to cut me off from any funds until I promised to mend my ways, or, at any rate, to make other friends?"

Amelia swept up the skirts of her riding habit with an impatient gesture. "I wondered that Mama could find the will to proceed against you in precisely the way she did," she said. "You are quite right, of course. Now that I think of it, I can see the duchess's hand in that, as well. I think we must defend ourselves against that woman before she interferes too much. I am prepared to be quite ruthless, I assure you. A little ruthlessness grounded in common sense is called for, I think."

She stopped as she said this last, halfway down the stairs, surprised to see her sister talking with a gentleman in the hall below. It was Lord Darrow, dressed as though he had just come from riding in the park in a bottle-green jacket of superfine and glistening Hessian boots. He turned and looked at her as she continued her descent of the stairs with Randolph behind her.

"I hope you will excuse an unexpected call, Miss Didright," he said.

"Lord Darrow has come to see Randolph," Elizabeth declared before he could continue, and Amelia knew that she was warning her not to think for an instant that he had come for any other purpose.

"I have just learned that your grandfather is ill," the young marquess said easily. "Let me convey my sympathies. I have often seen him sitting with Lord Queensberry when I passed down Piccadilly. He looked the sort of sprightly gentleman who would not enjoy being restricted to his bed."

Amelia was struck suddenly by a desire to tell him precisely what had happened and ask for his advice. But, of course, she could do nothing of the sort in the present situation. Indeed, before she could make any response, her mother came clattering down the stairs with the duchess proceeding more heavily behind her.

"My dear Lord Darrow!" Lady Didright cried. "What a delightful surprise!"

Amelia stared at her, bewildered. The last time her mother had encountered the marquess she had been quick to insult him. But now she saw that he was being greeted with smiles, and that even the duchess was beaming. Before she could begin to speculate on the reason for the change, they had all been whisked into the drawing room and her mother was ringing for tea.

"But, of course, my father is an old man, sir," Lady Didright was saying in response to Lord Darrow's repeated expression of sympathies. "It is only to be expected that something of the sort might happen. But he will be given the best of care, you may be certain of it."

"My personal physician is with him now," the duchess declared, taking her place in the most comfortable wing chair. "Elizabeth! Make room for Lord Darrow on the settee beside you. Yes. Just so! What a handsome pair you make. As I was saying, I have taken a personal responsibility as a dear friend of the family."

Amelia raged inside. How dare this woman

behave as though she were hostess here? If her mother had changed toward Lord Darrow it could only be because the duchess had something up her sleeve.

"Perhaps Lord Darrow has heard of the doctor in which we are to put so much stock," Amelia said. "His name is Pinchpurse."

"La, we must not talk of sickroom matters at such a time!" the duchess exclaimed. "It will not do at all! I hear that you had remarkable success recently at Newmarket, Lord Darrow. Does Elizabeth know that you delight in breeding horses? But of course you must have told her about that. I always think . . ."

"Do you know anything of Dr. Pinchpurse, sir?" Amelia repeated in a clear, firm voice.

"My dear!" her mother cried. "The duchess was speaking!"

Lord Darrow had not looked away from Amelia since she had voiced the question the first time and she thought, from the expression in his eyes, that he knew the question was far from being frivolous. Randolph was clearing his throat in embarrassment and Elizabeth was glowering to see her sister in center stage, but the marquess did not seem to notice.

"I have heard of him by reputation, Miss Didright," he replied.

"I only ask because my grandfather has never had a sick day in his life," Amelia replied. "And when I saw him last this morning he was full of energy. Of course he is old and cannot get about as quickly as he might wish, but I find it difficult to understand why he should be well one moment and suffering from any number of complaints the next. At least that is Dr. Pinchpurse's opinion. I think we should have another."

"Amelia!" Lady Didright cried. "I must insist that Lord Darrow not be troubled about such private matters! No! No response is needed, sir! You will displease me if you make one!"

"And you will displease *me,* sir," the duchess said archly, "if you will not agree to come to an entertainment at my house tomorrow evening. I think I can offer you as partner your companion on the settee. Come, Elizabeth! No need to turn your head away. A blush becomes you."

"Will you be there as well, Miss Didright?" Lord Darrow said, his eyes still on Amelia.

In the ordinary way of things, Amelia would have refused to set foot in the duchess's house, given the way she felt about her officious behavior. But she was determined to ask Lord Darrow about Dr. Pinchpurse and a variety of other things. She needed the counsel of someone who knew London well, she told herself. Something was going on which she did not fully understand, and she would arm herself in any way she could.

"Amelia does not care much for entertainments!" Lady Didright cried. "I declare, the child will be much happier here, tending to her grandfather."

It was a difficult position to have been put in, Amelia thought. There was nothing she wanted more dearly then to have an opportunity to talk to her grandfather alone. But what was to prevent the duchess and her mother with the assistance of

Dr. Pinchpurse to make that an impossibility even though not one of them was in the house? He had been drugged with laudanum today. He could be drugged in the same way tomorrow.

It was, she realized, necessary to make a quick decision. If what she suspected was true, her best chance to see her grandfather alone was at some time when no one suspected what she had in mind. Tonight, perhaps. Yes, that was it. She must not let them think they could manipulate her in any way.

"I cannot think why you would say I do not like entertainments, Mama," she said as lightly as she could. "Indeed, I dote on them, as you well know. And if the doctor continues to be as free with laudanum as he has been today, Grandpapa would doubtless be unaware of my presence in the house tomorrow night. Yes, Lord Darrow. I will be at the duchess's, and hope to see you there."

She saw the outraged look on her sister's face mirrored in the duchess's aristocratic visage. Or perhaps it was the other way around. Yes, she was certain of it now. Something was going on. And, willy-nilly, she meant to find out what it was.

Chapter 13

When Amelia tiptoed up the narrow stairs from the kitchen, the clock was striking midnight. A wind had risen outside at sunset, and odd corners of the house creaked and groaned ominously. Amelia did not notice. Catching her white, muslin dressing gown around her more tightly with one hand and raising the candle holder higher with the other, she opened the green baize door, which she had left ajar, by kicking it with a tiny, slippered foot. She took a deep breath when she saw that the main hall of the house was deserted. No one had heard her nocturnal ramblings, then. No one had deserted their bed to find out what was going on.

Amelia paused at the foot of the gracious, curving stairs which wound their way up into the darkness. The next step would involve the most risk. Had she been detected returning from the kitchen, she could have made the excuse of having wanted some warm milk and being just as willing to do it herself as wake one of the servants. It was not an absolutely convincing excuse, but it would have been adequate if she had needed to use it. After all, the fire in the kitchen hearth was kept banked all night. But it would not be so simple to provide a reason for a midnight visit to her grandfather's bedchamber where a woman hired specifically for the purpose was watching him.

Amelia was not certain that she would have had the courage to do this if Lord Darrow had not offered her encouragement of a sort by way of Randolph.

"He says that he would be obliged if you could see your way free to meet him at the stationers' on Bond Street tomorrow morning at eleven," her brother had told her when the young marquess had taken his leave. "He managed a word with me when I walked out with him. Tell me, Amelia, do you know what this is about? You are not the sort to have tête-à-têtes with someone like Darrow, surely."

Amelia had been aware of a sense of elation. He *had* taken what she had said seriously, then. He was no more content than she was to allow the duchess to decide who would speak to whom and when. And he was quite right to suggest such a meeting. The duchess was not to be trusted. If she was determined, for her own reasons, to keep Amelia and Lord Darrow at arm's length, she would doubtless find a way to do so at an entertainment in her own house. But this way she could meet the marquess as though by accident. Even Doris whom she would take along for a companion would not be the wiser.

She had explained it all truthfully enough to Randolph, reminding him that she had not been allowed a response the two times she had questioned Lord Darrow about whether he knew anything of Dr. Pinchpurse's reputation. "I think he has something to tell me about the man," she had said by way of explanation. "It is no real tête-à-tête. As you say, I am not the sort."

Her tone had been dry, but Randolph had taken what she said at face value, never suspecting irony. How well she had managed to create an image of a stay-at-home, Amelia told herself. What problems it seemed to present to so many people now that she had decided to change.

"There is really no need for you to sacrifice an evening with Grandpapa to go to a soirée at the duchess's," Elizabeth had said the instant the door had closed behind Lord Darrow and Randolph. "Indeed, even if a woman is brought in to care for him, I do not think that it is right that all of us should be out of the house at the same time. I must be there, of course. Lord Darrow will expect it. And Mama will only want to take part in the festivities, since I am being launched. It is her duty to see to the details of my coming-out."

The arguments had all been weak, but there had been so many of them that Amelia had turned on her heel to leave the drawing room.

"I really think you would be better off at home, my dear," she had heard her mother say.

But the final words had been those of the duchess. "You should show more consideration for your sister, Amelia," she said. "After all, it *is* her coming-out year and not your own. If she fancies Lord Darrow—and you *do*, Elizabeth! I can see you flush!—then she should have her try for him without distraction."

It had been that last which had persuaded Amelia that she would go to the duchess's house across the square, even though she would have seen Lord Darrow beforehand. She would not be manipulated. Beginning tonight. They had said her grandfather was sleeping and could not be disturbed at nine o'clock when the doctor had departed. Very well, she would make certain that she was beside him when he did awake.

Tiptoeing up the stairs, her candle throwing golden shadows around her, Amelia kept her ears open for any sound. But the house slept peacefully. At the top of the stairs, she turned to her grandfather's bedchamber further down the long passage. First tapping at the door, she gently opened it and saw her grandfather asleep, dwarfed by the pillows that had been propped behind his head. The candle on the table beside him, surrounded by bottles of pills and powders, was nearly gutted. The woman who had been hired to attend him sat beside the bed, legs spread apart, mobcapped head thrown to one side in a careless sort of way. She was snoring.

When Amelia shook her awake, none too gently, she was full of apology. "Why, Miss, I must have drifted off for a minute," she declared. "La, that has never happened before, I assure you! I'd take it as a favor if you would keep from mentioning it to Dr. Pinchpurse, that I would."

It was an opening of the sort Amelia had not dared to hope for. Perhaps her other ploy might not have to be mentioned after all. But when she expressed the desire to be informed the next time her grandfather awoke so that she could have a few minutes private conversation with him, the red-faced woman tucked her greasy hair up under her cap in a sluttish sort of way and assumed a sullen expression. It soon appeared that she had been particularly warned not to allow Lord Wellingham to have a private word with anyone during "his recovery."

"Except for Lady Didright, miss," the slattern went on. "That goes without saying. She was in here when he et his gruel at seven and spent a few minutes while he complained about his aches and pains."

It appalled Amelia that her mother had agreed to leave their grandfather in the care of a woman such as this, but she knew it would do no good to complain. No, she would see her removed from the house another way. In a quiet voice, she asked the creature for her name, and, having learned that it was Mrs. Bundy, she smiled in just such a way as to take the woman off her guard. And when she learned that there was waiting for her in the kitchen below a cold nuncheon, Mrs. Bundy hoisted herself out of her chair in very short order indeed.

"But who's to take a care of the old gentleman while I'm gone?" she said suspiciously.

"Why, I am, Mrs. Bundy," Amelia replied. "See how deep he sleeps. The laudanum you gave him— oh, yes, I know the doctor's orders—will not wear off for a while yet, will it?"

"He has another dose at two," the woman replied. "Perhaps if I was to fetch the food up here . . ."

But that did not suit Amelia at all. "I forgot to add that there is a bottle of gin set out with your cold chicken," she said. "You would not want to bring that up here, I think. And yet it is a shame to have a meal without it. I do not know what Mama was thinking about to imagine that you could go the night without some nourishment."

The mention of gin was enough to light a smoldering fire in Mrs. Bundy's eyes, just as Amelia had hoped it would. No doubt the woman did not lay claim to such a red nose for nothing.

"No need to hurry," Amelia said as the woman hurried out of the room. "You have nearly two hours before you need to give him his medicine again."

It had been a full bottle she had left for Mrs. Bundy's pleasure and, were she to drink it all, the time might well escape her. At least that was what Amelia hoped. Sitting beside her grandfather and stroking his forehead, she wondered if she had always been capable of being so unscrupulous. How could she blame her mother and the duchess for anything they did if she could be responsible for sending Mrs. Bundy to her fate?

But then she told herself that she had the greater good in mind and meant to hurt no one, suspecting that was a common argument. Still, if Mrs. Bundy *did* lose her job, she would not go untipped; for Amelia had taken care to slip two guineas in her apron pocket as the woman had passed her at the bottom of the bed.

She heard one o'clock strike, and directly afterward her grandfather's sleep ceased to be so deep. He tossed and turned his nightcapped head on the pillows, muttering unintelligible words, although once Amelia thought she heard him say her name. When two struck and Mrs. Bundy had not returned, Amelia bent close over the bed, watching and listening for any sign of the old man's awakening. At length his eyelids flickered. Flickered and then opened. Rheumy, blue eyes stared into hers.

"Grandpapa!" Amelia cried, pressing her cheek against his hollowed one. "Grandpapa!"

He spoke but his words ran together so in his toothless mouth that Amelia was forced to search about on the littered tables until she found his polished ivory teeth under a pile of linen. She helped him raise his head and put them in his mouth, and suddenly he looked so much himself that she felt faint with the relief of it.

"Damme!" were his first words, "If I was not so sick, I'd think that I was hungry, gel."

Never had any words been more welcome to Amelia's ears for she had come prepared to tempt him with delicacies. Detaching the reticule she had hung to the cord which circled her dressing gown at the waist, she opened it and took out napkin-wrapped biscuits of a special kind he liked, a boiled knuckle of veal which had been one of those served for dinner, and two plover's eggs which she had taken from the kitchen.

"I know you keep yourself a little store of claret up here, Grandpapa," she said when he was busy making a meal of it off the napkin. "For those occasions on which Mama decides to lock the cellar. Tell me where it is and I will fetch a bottle. Indeed, I may share it with you for I feel, some-how, as though I should celebrate a victory."

Later, with the fire poked into a blaze and her grandfather having declared himself replete, they sat in comfortable silence for a while. "Now, you must tell me how you feel," Amelia said finally. "You have no fever. I felt your forehead while you were asleep. If you ever had one, it has disap-peared and left no trace. And I took your pulse, as well. It is quite regular; for all that I could tell. But how are you inside yourself?"

"Damme, I scarcely know," the old man replied. The food and drink had brought some color to his cheeks and a sparkle to his eyes. "The doctor said that doubtless I should feel a numbing of the limbs, a cutting off of circulation. And palpita-tions here, just below my heart. Oh, yes. Short-ness of breath is to be expected, I believe he said. But to tell you the honest truth, gel, I would think that I felt in fine fettle if I did not know that the truth was precisely otherwise. I am a very sick man indeed."

"Nonsense!" Amelia cried. "They have only told you that because they wish you to believe it!"

"Give me that bottle, my dear," her grandfather said. "I will have another sip of it, although I believe I have had quite enough already. Why should they want me to believe that I am ill? Tell me that, then."

"I believe I set the change in motion," Amelia said thoughtfully, "when I decided to rebel. But I have not worked it out yet in my own mind. The important thing at present is to deal with your situation. I will tell you this. I believe Dr. Pinchpurse is a fraud. I mean to find out about his reputation tomorrow. Lord Darrow will help me, I think. He—he knows London so well that I have called on his opinion, at least."

"Lord Darrow, eh!" her grandfather replied with a return to some of his old liveliness. "Any excuse will do to take him in your confidence, what? I always said you were a clever gel."

"I truly think that he can help us, Grandpapa," Amelia insisted. "I do not think he is any more taken in by the duchess than I am, at any rate, and he knows this world for what it is."

"So do I, gel. So do I," the old man said in a graver manner. "And I do not fancy being confined to bed, I can tell you that. But what am I to do? You say that I am well and, damme, I hope that you are right. But when the doctor says that I may be at death's door and describes the symptoms, I find I do not feel as well as I ought. I'm an old man, child. I could go off at any instant in a stroke."

He shivered at the thought of it and raised the claret bottle to his lips once more. It came to Amelia that perhaps she had not been wise in giving him his tipple. She would never forgive herself if he should do himself a damage because of her. And yet she knew she must believe that she was right or he would remain on here in his bed, slowly growing weaker.

"At any rate, you must not allow anyone to dose you," she said. "The doctor is too fond of laudanum, I think. You can turn stubborn and close your lips. Or spit it out when no one is looking. Do what you can to resist until I have seen Lord Darrow tomorrow, at any rate. With luck I can discover proof that Dr. Pinchpurse is a fraud and confront Mama with it."

At just that moment the door to the bedchamber opened and Mrs. Bundy appeared. Her complexion was an even higher color than it had been before and her nose was like a purple plum. She carried a gin bottle in one hand and a chickenleg in the other as she moved gingerly into the room and stared about her with glazed eyes. And then, finding a wall to lean against, she slowly slid down to the floor in a sitting position and fell into what could most kindly be called a slumber.

"Your nurse, Grandpapa," Amelia said dryly as Mrs. Bundy's snores rent the air. "Never mind. I can sleep quite comfortably in this chair. Now, you must get some rest. No need for laudanum, I think. And in the morning we will set about putting things right."

Chapter 14

Bond Street was not as crowded in a morning as it was by afternoon, but it was still necessary to walk very close to the bow-windowed shops in order to avoid the carriages which jammed the narrow streets. It had been raining earlier and Amelia was forced to hold the tamboured hem of her blue muslin morning gown in order to keep it from touching the wet cobblestones. She wore a dark blue cape, as well, and a simple *dormeuse* bonnet trimmed with a ribbon to match, for she wished to make a point of the fact that this was nothing to her but the most casual encounter.

"I declare, miss," Doris complained as they were forced to press themselves up against the wall of a draper's shop in order to avoid collision with a passing barouche, "I wonder we did not leave our carriage at wherever it is you intend to shop. This is no day for walking in the street."

"Don't fuss," Amelia replied absently as she turned in at the stationers' door and beckoned to her abigail to follow. "Mind you remember what I told you on the way here. Elizabeth is not to be given any description of whatever it is that may happen this morning."

"I never was a one to gossip," Doris replied. "And well you know it, miss. Although why Miss Elizabeth would care about your coming here I'm certain that I have no notion."

With that she followed Amelia through the door, a plump and pretty miss with fresh country color still on her cheeks. Elizabeth had been in favor of taking on another abigail for their stay in the city, someone who "knows London ways," she said. But Doris had begged to accompany them and Amelia, who was genuinely fond of her, had insisted. Now she wondered if Doris would be shocked if she knew that one of her mistresses had planned a tête-à-tête.

But Lord Darrow did not appear to be waiting for her and, for a moment, Amelia's heart sank. Had Randolph got the message wrong? Had the young marquess changed his mind? She could not blame him if he had decided, having given the matter further thought, that he did not wish to become entangled in her family affairs. And then, looking at the watch which she kept hanging from her belt, she saw that she was early.

Commissioning Lucy to choose her some writing paper, Amelia made a pretense of looking at quills and sealing wax at the very back of the shop where the smell of ink and parchment was particularly strong. Her thoughts trailed back to the morning when Mrs. Bundy had been discovered, still reclined against the wall, the gin bottle clutched in her hand.

"I cannot think how such a thing could have happened!" Lady Didright had exclaimed as she sat between her two daughters in their sitting room. "I dismissed her on the spot, of course, and I shall want to question Dr. Pinchpurse very closely indeed to find out how he could recommend such a jade to me."

Amelia pretended to be shocked, although there had not been time for that particular emotion to settle in her breast. She had sat with her grandfather through the night, sleeping when he slept. Early in the morning when the servants began to stir in their small rooms overhead, she had whispered her last words of encouragement to her grandfather, hidden the empty claret bottle in the closet and taken her departure, stepping over Mrs. Bundy's turned-out feet to do so.

The outcry had begun soon afterward when one of the maids had opened the door to Lord Wellingham's room, a mop in one hand and a dustcloth in the other. Elizabeth, however, slept too heavily to hear anything and Amelia thought it was the better part of wisdom to pretend she did the same. Her only need for real concern might be that Mrs. Bundy would confide the source of her refreshment. But now it seemed that she had preferred attack to apology, or explanation.

"You cannot imagine what she said to me!" Lady Didright had told her daughters. "The words she used! La, but I never heard anything of the sort before! Of course your grandfather was amused. Poor man. He tries to pretend that he is the same as he ever was. But it is all up with him, I am afraid. His active days are over. I tried to tell him so, but he turned awkward and demanded liver and sausage for his breakfast. He'd managed somehow to get his false teeth in and nothing I could say or do would get them out. Of course, the doctor will see to it that he behaves. But I was so annoyed with him, not to mention that dreadful woman, that I left him with the scullery maid for his companion."

"And liver and sausage for breakfast?" Amelia had asked. "It would help to keep up his strength better than the gruel the doctor advises."

"Oh, dear, I do not think that I should interfere with the diet the doctor prescribes!" Lady Didright exclaimed. "It is a great responsibility to have his entire welfare in my hands."

"No need to make a fuss, Mama!" Elizabeth said impatiently. "If Grandpapa's health is standing in the way of my completing my Season as I ought, of course it will be quite another matter. But all you need do now is follow the doctor's orders and get another woman to attend to him."

It had been difficult for Amelia to resist the temptation to tell her sister, straight out, that she was a selfish, mean-hearted chit. What a fool she had been to have treated Elizabeth like a wayward child for so many years. A few days ago she had been willing to blame herself for the way her younger sister behaved, but now she was determined not to take full responsibility. She may have been the go-between her mother had chosen and, as a consequence, most often the arbiter of Elizabeth's ways, but that was the end of it. From the first moment she had opened her mouth as a little child, her sister had made it clear that she thought of nothing or no one beside herself, and she was still doing so.

"I hope you will be more careful in your next choice of nurse, Mama," Amelia said in a low voice.

She was the doctor's choice, not mine!" Lady Didright exclaimed, jumping from her seat and beginning to dart hither and thither about the room as she always did when she was nervous. "You cannot blame me for what happened, my dear. Surely not! How was I to know the woman was too fond of gin by far?"

"It is a mystery to me how she knew where to find Cook's bottle," Elizabeth said slowly, weaving her fingers through her golden curls. "We all know that Cook keeps her tipple in the larder, but I do not understand how a perfect stranger could, apparently, have gone straight to it."

"No doubt she smelled it out," Amelia said dryly, "just as hounds smell game."

It struck her that she must be on the way to becoming a great cynic not to care more than she did about Mrs. Bundy's fate. Thanks to her the woman had lost her position. But, if she was one of Dr. Pinchpurse's "nurses," no doubt she should have another position promptly. Not only did Amelia suspect that his patients seldom got well, but that most of the assistants he recommended were of Mrs. Bundy's caliber. Furthermore, she had been a dreadful creature, there was no mistaking that, not the sort of person who should ever have been left with an old man who believed himself to be helpless. No, she could not be sorry about Mrs. Bundy's fate.

Now, fingering a glass blotter full of sand, Amelia remembered that she had challenged her mother.

"The woman was irresponsible," she had said. "And Dr. Pinchpurse recommended her. Doesn't that make you wonder about him, Mama? I declare it makes me wonder a great deal."

"Oh dear! Oh dear! I wish dear Dorelle would arrive!" Lady Didright had fussed, darting to the window in her sparrow's way and looking out. "She braces me, indeed she does."

"As for that, Mama," Amelia had said. "I think you are becoming as dependent on the duchess as Mrs. Bundy is on gin. Pardon me. I do not mean to be impertinent, but I cannot understand why it is that you refuse to discuss the matter of Dr. Pinchpurse."

"Perhaps she refuses because there is nothing to discuss!" Elizabeth said pertly, also rising. In her yellow and white gauzy gown, standing in a pool of sunlight, she looked a perfect picture, or would have had it not been for the way she frowned. "The duchess recommended him. That is quite enough for me. It is enough for Mama. And, if you were not determined to be troublesome, it would be enough for you! But you can never believe that anyone but you could possibly make a wise decision! Now that Mama chooses to trust someone else's decisions, nothing will do but you must prove the duchess wrong!"

Amelia decided to ignore her. "Mama," she said. "All that I am asking is that you agree to consult another physician as well as Dr. Pinchpurse."

"Dear Dorelle says that it will not do to appear to mistrust him!" Lady Didright exclaimed, darting away from the window. "She is coming now, for I just saw her entering the square. Try to persuade her, Amelia. There is nothing I can do."

Amelia took her mother's hands and held them tight. "You behave as though you cannot think for yourself, Mama," she murmured. "Why should I argue anything with the duchess? She is not a member of our family. Certainly she is not the head of it. But *you* are. You must remember that. If *you* believe that Dr. Pinchpurse should attend Grandpapa . . ."

"Oh, I do! I do!" Lady Didright had exclaimed, backing toward the door. "Come now! I think I hear the duchess on the stairs. I do not want her to find us arguing. Why, she already believes . . . But no matter!"

And before Amelia had been able to stop her, she had been out the door and halfway down the stairs.

"I do not blame Mama for running away from you if you insist on nagging so," Elizabeth said petulantly. "I do not know why you should turn so havey-cavey over the fact that Grandpapa has taken to his bed."

"He has not *taken* to it," Amelia had told her grimly. "He has been *put* there. And there is a difference, Elizabeth, although it may well be asking too much of you to see it."

Thus it was that when Amelia had left the house with Doris in tow, Elizabeth had not only failed to suggest that she go shopping with them, but had, in fact, turned her back when Amelia appeared.

"Miss Elizabeth needs a sound scold," Doris had said as they left the house. "There, I expect you will tell me it is none of my business, Miss Amelia, and no doubt it is not! But she is either sour or sullen, with no sweet in between."

"Have I ever told you something was not your business?" Amelia had asked her as they paused outside the door. "I did her no favor in the past to put up with her sulks, and I have determined to take a different course from now on."

Doris had stared at her then in a puzzled sort of way and, looking up, Amelia saw the reason for her abigail's confusion.

"Thank you for coming, Miss Didright," Lord Darrow said in a low voice. "I hope you did not think me impertinent to ask to see you."

He was handsome, as usual, wearing the riding clothes which suited him to perfection. In the shadows at the back of the shop where they were standing, his eyes were very dark indeed.

"Will you make a choice of some note paper for me, Doris?" Amelia asked and silence fell between her and Lord Darrow until the abigail had made her way to the front of the shop.

"I see that I have put you in an awkward situation," Lord Darrow murmured with a smile.

"There is no awkwardness," Amelia told him. "My abigail is to be trusted."

Lord Darrow's eyes grew somber. "It is as I suspected then," he said. "Some intrigue is going on."

Amelia looked at him thoughtfully, wondering why it was so difficult to order her thoughts. Last night she had meant to go over what she was to say, but then the business of Mrs. Bundy had put everything but her grandfather out of her mind. She had not even considered how much or little she would tell this gentleman.

"I cannot be certain," she replied, deciding to be as straightforward with him as possible. "It is true that lately my mother has changed. First she took one extraordinary step involving my brother, and now it seems she has let the duchess persuade her that my grandfather needs the care of a physician."

Lord Darrow's eyes were intense. They never left her face. "You do not think that he is ill, then?"

Quickly, in as few words as possible, Amelia told him of the circumstances under which the old man had been discovered to be suffering from every known disease.

"And yet not two hours before that, my brother and I had encountered him at Lord Queensberry's and my grandfather set off alone to settle matters between Mama and Randolph, quite full of energy. He is very lame, of course, and frail in some ways. But I have never known him to have an ill day in his life and now he is suddenly an invalid who will never be allowed to stray further than Portman Square as long as we are in London. That is why I wanted to know what you had heard of Dr. Pinchpurse."

"The duchess was determined that you would not get an answer from me," Lord Darrow replied. "You must have noticed. I could have insisted on giving you your answer, but I did not know the situation and was not certain of the consequences if I were to condemn the charlatan out of hand."

Amelia caught her breath. "Is—is that what you are prepared to do now, sir?" she demanded. "Do you know something against him?"

"Everything I know about the fellow speaks against him," Lord Darrow said. "I can find you a score of people who will substantiate the fact that he is a quack. If the Duchess of Bradlaw recommended him, she must have a purpose something other than your grandfather's well-being."

Forgetting herself, Amelia put her hand on his arm and saw his expression change. Quickly she pulled her gloved fingers away, but it had been done. A trace of intimacy lingered between them.

"Will you speak to Mama about it?" Amelia said quickly. "I know she would not do Grandpapa any harm deliberately. But she has come to trust the duchess overmuch. I blame myself for that because . . . But then, it does not matter."

Lord Darrow's eyes did not move from her face.

The very intensity of his gaze was disturbing. "I think perhaps you blame yourself for too many things, Miss Didright," he said. "But, as you say, that is beside the point. Of course I will speak to your mother. I can give her the names of some people she might like to contact if she does not like to take my word that the fellow is a cheat."

"Speak to her tonight, then," Amelia told him. Over his shoulder she could see that Doris was looking at her curiously still. "At the duchess's soirée."

"Would it not be best for me to see her alone at her own house, Miss Didright?" the marquess said slowly. "I am prepared to return there with you now."

"No, no!" Amelia said too quickly.

The dark eyes narrowed. "It would not do to let your family know that you had spoken to me privately, I see. Very well. I will take that on trust and not ask why. At the duchess's, it will be."

"Speak to my mother when she is alone," Amelia said, flashing him a grateful smile. "If the duchess is with her, she will find some way to intervene. Only tell Mama what you have told me and I am certain that she will see the light."

Lord Darrow smiled as he bent to kiss her hand in the Continental fashion. "You are a curious blend of naiveté and cynicism, Miss Didright," he murmured. "I declare that you intrigue me."

Later Amelia knew that he must have been poking gentle fun of her, but for a moment the expression in his eyes so startled her that she pulled her fingers away from his and pressed them to her lips in a gesture of surprise.

"The gentleman is a casual acquaintance, Doris," she said a moment later when he was gone. "He intends to do a slight favor for me. There is nothing more to it than that."

Amelia spoke with great conviction. After all, she would be a great fool indeed to think that a roué like Lord Darrow did not know of a hundred ways to charm a lady straight up from the country. Doubtlessly he would be sharing the encounter with Hanger or Berkeley within the hour at their club.

"No, there is nothing to it at all," she said to the abigail and tried her best to be content to believe it.

Chapter 15

By evening Amelia had nearly decided not to go to the duchess's soirée after all, much to Elizabeth's delight.

"Since neither Mama nor Dr. Pinchpurse has been able to find an attendant for Grandpapa who meets with your approval," Elizabeth said spitefully, "you must pay the penalty and sit with him yourself."

It had been a harrowing day in many ways. First there had been the meeting with Lord Darrow which should have been reassuring since she had enlisted his help. Instead, Amelia had come away disconcerted, aware that something had passed between her and Lord Darrow that neither of them were prepared to accept.

Arriving home, she had found not only her mother but the duchess, as well, in her grandfather's bedchamber, arguing with the old man who was bound and determined to be up and about.

"I want some solid food," he was demanding when Amelia entered the room. "Damme, if you persist in starving me to death, I'll have the law on you, gel, even if you are my daughter."

Lady Didright flushed, and murmured something about following the doctor's orders, but the duchess hove into the fray with her customary vigor. According to her, Dr. Pinchpurse had never made a mistaken diagnosis. Furthermore, she had known of many cases like Lord Wellingham's on her own account, and solid food was bound to send him into a decline. Whereupon the old man had bounced up and down on the mattress in his fury and declared that he had suffered no ill effects from the cold knuckle of veal Amelia had brought him the night before, not to mention the claret.

It had been at that awkward moment that Amelia's presence in the doorway had been noted. Both the duchess and her mother had advanced on her, demanding an explanation.

"You had a hand in seeing that Mrs. Bundy drank herself into her cups!" the duchess declared, towering over Amelia in a disconcerting way and pointing an accusatory finger. "I wondered about that at the time. Dr. Pinchpurse assured me that he would personally see that she did not have any gin in her possession when she came into the house."

"So!" Amelia cried. "You and he both knew that she was unreliable, Madam! Were you aware of that as well, Mama?"

"Dear Dorelle," Lady Didright said, looking up at her imposing friend with her face knotted into a frown, "you should have told me. You know I would not risk my own father to the care of someone I could not trust."

"You are being taken advantage of, my dear Selina," the duchess replied. "Your eldest daughter is a manipulator of events. For some reason she has taken it into her mind to thwart your attempt to provide your father with proper care. And so she tempts a poor, unfortunate woman to make a toffle of herself."

"I did not tempt her to fall alseep in *that* chair beside *that* bed," Amelia declared, her cheeks burning. "Which was precisely what she was doing when I came to look in on Grandpapa last night. She was a dirty, miserable creature who should never have been allowed inside this house. Come to your senses, Mama! I beg you, do! There is nothing wrong with Grandpapa. He would be better off with a solid meal under his belt and sent off to Piccadilly to see Lord Queensberry!"

She had spoken with so much feeling that the tears had come into her eyes and her throat had choked. For a moment her mother had put her arms around her and Amelia had dared to hope the older woman had been touched. And then Dr. Pinchpurse himself had appeared with his long arms and crooked nose and air of authority. Lady Didright had capitulated at once.

"I see, I see," the doctor said when the duchess had finished telling him about Amelia's escapade of the night before. "There's nothing like head-strong gels to cause a bit of trouble. But we shall put it right, my dear duchess. Ah ha! The patient is sitting up, I see. And he has his teeth in, as well! What nonsense is this, Lord Wellingham? Have you a special fondness for becoming a corpse as soon as possible? It can be arranged, you know. Oh, yes. It can be arranged. All that is necessary is that I let you continue to behave like a gammon."

It was the first time Amelia had ever heard a social inferior address her grandfather in what was certainly an impertinent manner. Apparently it was Dr. Pinchpurse's philosophy that disease and old age robbed a man of his dignity as readily as a thief might rob him of his money. She held her breath, waiting for the explosion which was sure to come. Her grandfather might allow Lord Queensberry to call him a gammon, but very few other people might, and certainly the doctor was not among them.

But instead of falling into a rage, the old man seemed to crumple against the pillows. And, it was true that a certain air of mastery clung to the doctor. He seemed to make a point of demonstrating his relative youth and vigor as a contrast which could not be ignored. Amelia's grandfather made no protest when Dr. Pinchpurse looked into his eyes, pulling the eyelids up with no particular gentleness.

"Tut, tut!" he said as he bent to place his ear against the old man's chest. "Something has gone amiss here! My orders have not been followed!"

Even though Amelia knew that he might well have overheard the conversation which had preceded his entry into the room and based his remarks on foreknowledge rather than any symptoms he might or might not perceive, she found herself listening anxiously. Lord Darrow had told her that this man was a fraud, but could she trust him? Was it just possible that her grandfather's life *was* in danger? She would hate to think that anything she might have done would put him at any risk.

"Miss Didright took it upon herself to provide her grandfather with just the sort of solid food you have forbidden him," the duchess said. "And you might be interested to know that poor Mrs. Bundy was deliberately made a pawn, for this gel has as good as admitted, by her reluctance to make a direct reply, that she tempted her with gin, sir. She *made* her drunk!"

"Yes!" Amelia exclaimed, looking at the duchess defiantly. "And I will find some way to remove any other disreputable person of that sort from this house if the doctor brings another in."

Dr. Pinchpurse ignored her in a lordly manner. "Give me your teeth, sir," he said to Lord Wellingham. "Give them to me or I will take them out myself. If you have a convulsion, there is no knowing what would happen with them still in your mouth."

Not able to see or hear anymore, without losing control altogether, Amelia had whirled out of the room and blindly pushed past her brother and sister as they came along the corridor. Once in her own bedchamber, she had thrown herself onto the quilt and wept out of sheer frustration. Never had a defeat left so bitter a taste in her mouth.

"I declare, miss, you shouldn't cry like that," she heard Doris say a few minutes later after the door had been gently opened and closed. "You'll spoil your eyes for tonight, indeed you will."

At that Amelia had declared that she cared nothing for the appearance of her eyes and that she did not intend to go to the duchess's house in any event. "I must see to it that no one who does not have my trust is allowed to care for Grandpapa," she said. Whereupon she had tidied her black curls and dashed cold water on her eyes before returning to her grandfather's room and taking a seat in the corner where she had declared she would remain until a responsible nurse had been found.

Thus it was that when evening came and the matter was, at last, resolved, with Doris promising to watch over the old man as carefully as she would a babe, that Amelia was nearly too dispirited to want to attend any soirée, particularly one at the duchess's house. Granted that she had won one battle, but she had lost another for nothing she could do or say had been enough to dissuade the doctor from administering such a dose of laudanum that her grandfather had not stirred all day.

"If he wakes while I am gone, do not give him another dose, as the doctor ordered," Amelia had whispered to her abigail before she left the house. "With any luck Mama will be persuaded that Dr. Pinchpurse is not fit to care for him and, if another doctor is to examine him, he should find Grandpapa with an unclouded mind."

With her grandfather on her mind, Amelia found it was impossible to view the evening expectantly, but Elizabeth did not suffer accordingly. Both she and Amelia had chosen to wear simple, white polonaise gowns, although Elizabeth's was plentifully decorated with green and yellow ribbons and furbelows and she wore thin-woven yellow stockings, not to mention yellow shoes with high wedge heels. During the ride around the square to the duchess's house, she talked constantly, first complaining that Amelia was taking more than her share of the seat and then anticipating the pleasures of the evening.

"Poor Randolph!" she declared, patting her brother's knee. "None of your good friends will be there. Except for Lord Darrow, of course. The duchess made a point of telling me that she would make an exception in his case because of me. But otherwise there will not be a rake in sight! She did that for you, Mama. She told me so herself."

"Yes, dear Dorelle is a fine friend," Lady Didright said with a sigh. Ever since the contretemps concerning her father, she had been pensive and inclined to brood at odd moments. Amelia was not certain of her mother's precise mood, but she hoped it was one in which she would be predisposed to listen to what Lord Darrow had to tell her.

"Mama intends to give me the money to pay off my wager with Hanger tomorrow," Randolph said dolefully as he and Amelia tagged behind their mother and sister on the grand stairway of the duchess's house on Curzon Street. "As soon as I take it from her, the bargain will be made. I wish there had been some other way."

"Perhaps if you told Mr. Hanger the conditions, he would be willing to wait until you reach your majority," Amelia suggested. But Randolph shook his head.

"Mama may call people like Hanger and Berkeley rakes and scoundrels, but they are exceedingly honorable in the matter of paying wagers of this sort. There is a particular sort of honor involved, of the variety which allows them to keep tradesmen waiting but not their friends."

It was, Amelia thought gloomily, a very grand occasion indeed. Footmen in white and gold livery lined the curved stairs, standing very upright, like soldiers. At the top the duchess stood, greeting the guests who had first been announced by a butler with a booming voice. Beside the duchess stood a little man who came approximately to her elbow. Rotund and sad of eye, he fidgeted with his richly embroidered waistcoat when he was not greeting guests and shifted back and forth on his tiny, slippered feet as though such entertainments were not much to his liking. Amelia had never met the Duke of Bradlaw. Indeed, the duchess never seemed to speak of him. The girl felt a wave of pity for him as she accepted his greeting. Beside him the duchess was greeting an embarrassed Randolph with a fulsome embrace.

"Dear boy!" Amelia heard her announce to anyone who happened to be listening. "I feel as though you were part of my own family. Indeed I do!"

"Why on earth did Mama take up with that woman?" Randolph muttered between his teeth when he had been released and he and Amelia were making their way into the crowded ballroom.

"What's worse," she told him, "is that I suspect she is behind a good deal of our difficulties. I believe that Mama is taking her advice in everything, which may explain why you should suddenly find yourself having to beg and bargain for funds, as well as why it is that Grandpapa must become an invalid."

Randolph cried out in pain as a hearty lady wearing a towering white wig on top of which was set a model of a ship in full sail moved backward and, in so doing, stepped heavily on his toe. Indeed, the crowd was now so thick that Amelia wondered how there could be dancing. Her mother and Elizabeth had disappeared and it seemed quite likely that Randolph would be separated from her, too, unless steps were taken to prevent it.

And then Lord Darrow appeared out of nowhere, his classic features set in grim lines as he, like they, was buffeted about by the crowd. This evening he was dressed like a dandy with a sky-blue silk embroidered coat and scarlet waistcoat and his dark hair was thickly powdered, making his

face seem bronzed. Suddenly Amelia wished that
she was not so simply dressed. She had told herself, a week ago, that she would cease to be of such
a serious turn of mind. Yet here she was, wrapped
up in private worries. She realized she had even
gone so far as to make her relationship with Lord
Darrow, slight as it was, into a very serious one.
At her request he was to apply this very evening
to her mother in an attempt to persuade her to
call in another doctor. It had been kind of him to
offer to do it, surely, but he must think her very
intense, the serious sort. Burdened by common
sense. Oh, it had been foolish of her to think that
she could change her colors! Even now Lord Darrow was doing her a service. With him at one side
and Randolph at the other, a way was being
plowed through the duchess's guests toward a safe
alcove.

"Dash it, Darrow, that is what one could call a
crush!" Randolph exclaimed when they stood together in the shelter of red velvet curtains. "I
thought you never came to stodgy affairs like
this."

"Not a very exciting gathering, I agree," the
young marquess said with a smile. "Present company excepted, of course. I confess to loathing
these affairs."

"And yet you are here," Randolph replied.

"To excute a commission," Lord Darrow said,
his eyes lingering on Amelia's face. "And for one
other reason besides. But that does not explain
your presence, sir."

"It is either company like this from now on, or no company at all," Randolph replied. Clearly he meant to make a full confession of his plight, but just then an imperious-looking lady swathed in a particularly bilious shade of green silk tapped his shoulder with her fan and informed him that his mother had said that he would be delighted to dance with her daughter who was waiting just over there. Amelia saw her brother's face fall as a giggling damsel with very little to recommend her as for appearance was pointed out to him. In the distance the sound of violins tuning could be heard and Randolph was led in that direction with the air of a man going to his execution.

"Your brother does not often pride himself in being an enigma," Lord Darrow said, "but I confess that I do not understand his last remark."

It was a time for frankness, Amelia knew. Nothing could be easier than for her to confide in him and she would reap the added intimacy of a confidential relationship. But something inside her held her back. She had already asked him to help her with one family problem. Yes. By asking his opinion of Dr. Pinchpurse she had deliberately involved him. Now, if she told him of the constraints which her mother was putting on Randolph's activities, she would be as good as asking him, as her brother's friend, to think of possible solutions, to offer advice. He would come to associate her with problems. No doubt he already did. The only reason he was talking to her now was that he was, no doubt, about to approach her mother and had wanted a few words with her first.

"You must ask Randolph, sir," Amelia said and was shocked to find how cold it sounded. "I mean to say, it is his story and . . ."

"You do not need to explain, Miss Didright," Lord Darrow said rather stiffly. "Believe me, it was not my intent to pry. The dancing is about to start at any moment, I believe. I will try to talk privately with your mother now and let you know what we have said. Then there is another engagement I must honor, another party at another place."

It was as though he had said that he would deal with her tiresome problem as early in the evening as possible because he wanted to get away from what was, for him, a tiresome event. Amelia's cheeks stung and she knew that she was blushing.

"I assure you that there is no need for you to speak to my Mama, sir," she said in a cold, clear voice. "No doubt the situation involving my grandfather will resolve itself quite satisfactorily without your help. Indeed, I must beg you not to waste further time here in this—this dreadful crush."

For a moment Lord Darrow did not speak. "I am not the sort who cares to shift course in midstream," he said finally. "I came here to speak to your mother and I will do so. And if, somehow, I have led you to think that I am currying some special attention from you, pray do not be misled. I can be altruistic, you see. Rogues sometimes are, I understand."

And with that parting shot he disappeared into the crowd. Or rather, because of his height, he did not quite disappear for awhile. Amelia watched him until he did.

Chapter 16

Knowing that she could not face Lord Dar-
row again that evening, no matter what he had to
report after talking to her mother, Amelia took
refuge in a corner of the room where, despite the
crowds, she could see something of what was
happening. She had lost sight of the marquess for
awhile, now she saw him making his way toward
the gilt chairs which lined the wall where Lady
Didright was sitting with all the other matrons.

The conversation took only a few minutes and
Amelia could not make out the expression on her
mother's face when it came to a conclusion. But
she did see Lord Darrow turn and scan the room.
No doubt he was in a hurry to tell her about her
mother's response and be gone to join livelier
company. Amelia's cheeks stung again and she
turned and fled through one ornately furnished

salon after another until she came to a shadowy library where she hid herself, pretending to read by the light of a dying fire until she was certain he must have given over searching for her and be gone.

True enough, that was what had happened. Elizabeth, whom Amelia met soon after emerging from her lair, made a point of it.

"I cannot think why Lord Darrow should have left so abruptly!" she explained petulantly. "First he was here and then he was gone. I was on the dance floor when I saw him going out the door and, as a consequence, could do nothing to prevent him."

Randolph, joining them, declared that, since he had left Amelia talking to the young marquess, she might know the answer.

"I should have guessed!" Elizabeth exclaimed. "Of course you were responsible, Amelia! You knew that the duchess invited Lord Darrow particularly for me! What was it you told him? That I had saved all my dances for another gentleman? La, you have always been jealous of me, but I have never known you to be so vindictive!"

The duchess chose this moment to appear on the scene, red-faced and puffing, with Lady Didright in her wake.

"It must be that someone offended him," she said looking at Amelia in a pointed sort of way. " 'You can't be leaving us so early, Lord Darrow!' I said when he came to say his goodbye. 'Why, you have not danced a single dance and I know a certain young lady who will be more than willing to oblige you.' "

"He probably thought you meant Amelia," Elizabeth said spitefully. "Don't you see? He was making his escape."

Amelia scarcely heard them. Her attention was focused on her mother. There was a troubled look in Lady Didright's brown eyes and it was clear that she was not attending to what was being said. Amelia wondered whether Lord Darrow had succeeded in convincing her that Dr. Pinchpurse should not attend her father. She told herself that if he had succeeded it would be well worth enduring the fiasco which this evening was rapidly becoming. After all, what did it matter to her whether he went or stayed? And as for Elizabeth's insults, she did not care one way or the other for them.

"Come, Selina!" the duchess was demanding. "What did Lord Darrow talk to you about? It seemed a serious enough discussion. I tried to join you but the crush was simply too great. I cannot imagine how I came to invite so many people! Why, it was all that I could do to intercept Lord Darrow by the doorway, and then he was off and away so quickly that there was no time for asking questions."

Lady Didright did not answer. Indeed, she did not appear to have heard the duchess. Instead, she was staring at Amelia and, presently, she took her elder daughter's arm.

"I would have a word with you in private, my

dear," she said in a low voice. "Something Lord Darrow said . . ."

It was at that moment that pandemonium broke loose. At first all that was apparent was that ladies were screaming and gentlemen were making gruff exclamations. And then the crowd began to shift like sand on a beach when a wave strikes it. And then, quite suddenly, a path appeared directly before Amelia and the others, a path which led straight to the main floor of the ballroom. And down that path came, whirling and tumbling, a motley crew of both sexes, the gentlemen wearing masks to resemble bears and tigers and the ladies, of which there were two, guised as cats complete with whiskers. One of the bears brought a flute to his mouth when he had reached the center of the dance floor and began to play a merry tune to which his masked friends proceeded to cavort.

"Scandalous!" the duchess exclaimed. "I must put a stop to this at once! The duke will do nothing, of course. He never does!"

"Dear, dear Dorelle," Lady Didright cried, "I really think that you should not! It is quite inexcusable, of course! Quite shocking! But if you let them have their little fling, they will leave quietly, no doubt."

It did not seem likely to Amelia that such would be the case, for the flutist had launched into another tune this one so merry that one of the violinists in the little orchestra the duchess had employed was tempted to join in. As for the company in general, they had gone from shock to bewilderment and back to shock again. True there were no more screams or other signs of hysteria, although fans were being waved with considerable abandon. Face after face wore an expression of disapproval. For the first time since she had arrived, Amelia noticed that the general age of the duchess's company was rather closer to fifty than not, and that what young people there were on hand were characterized by dour features and undistinguished dress. In the midst of them the gaily-dressed revelers, with their fantastic masks, might have come from another world.

Lady Didright did not desist in her arguments until it became clear that the duchess could not be restrained a moment longer. As she made her way down the path which led to the revelers, a hush settled on the company in which the flute, in perfect harmony now with the violin, could be heard with crystal clarity. Around and around the masked dancers sped.

"It's Lord Darrow and his friends!" Amelia heard Elizabeth murmur. "I know it is!"

"It would be just as well if you did not allow Mama to hear you say that," Randolph reminded her in a low voice.

"Besides, I think it quite unlikely that he would lend himself to this display," Amelia retorted.

"Of course *you* would disapprove," Elizabeth retorted. "I can understand why the duchess is upset, but, I declare . . ."

"Oh dear!" Lady Didright wailed. "I warned her to leave them alone. Only look! They've taken her by the arms and made her dance with them! Oh,

poor, dear Dorelle, to be made a mock of in her
own ballroom!"

And indeed the duchess had become a sight as,
skirts billowing and her turban tilted to one side
in such a way as to make the feathers appear to
languish, she was whirled from one dancer to
another. Around and around she went, her lips set
in a perfect circle and her eyes bulging from their
sockets.

"The shame of it!" Lady Didright cried. "The
perfect shame of it!"

Amelia was torn between a desire to laugh and
a sense of dismay. If it had not been for Elizabeth's suggestion that Lord Darrow might be one
of the masked figures, she might have been amused
and nothing more. But the very notion that he
might have deliberately schemed to humiliate his
hostess in such a way appalled her. Which meant,
she could not help but suppose, that she was
always to be a victim of her own conservatism.
But no. It was not that precisely. It was only that
she had thought of Lord Darrow in a very particular way, a way which did not match this wild
performance. And yet, one of the masked gentlemen was about his height and wore a satin jacket
of the same shade of blue and a scarlet waistcoat.
Surely that was too much of a coincidence. And
yet she still could not believe . . .

The dance was over for the duchess, Amelia
observed. The flute and violin still sang, but one
gentleman with the head of a shaggy bear, was
escorting the lady to a seat where he deposited her
with all due alacrity to return to his friends. But

there was to be no more dancing. Instead they began to make their way down the paths which led to the door, not running, as one might have thought they would, but looking this way and that through the slant eyes of their masks. Amelia was aware of a sudden sense of foreboding and, at that very moment, her arms were caught by the two ladies wearing cats' heads and she was being pulled to the stairs and down them, thinking of nothing but how to keep her balance. Cries rang out behind them and Amelia could distinctly hear Randolph shout her name. And then they were in the street and she was being half helped, half carried into a covered carriage which was set in motion in an instant. Before she could believe what was happening, Amelia was being driven through London streets in the company of two giggling revelers and one tiger-faced gentleman.

She could not make out where they were going through the canvas-flap window closest her, but she thought it was in the direction of St. James's where the Prince lived in splendor at Carlton House. The thought that he might have been involved struck Amelia as just as unbelievable as everything else which had happened this evening. She had been severely startled to be abducted, but she was not alarmed. Anger? Yes, there was that. Because of the sheer arrogance of what they were doing.

One of the ladies began to speak, but the other hushed her instantly. Apparently they were to reach their destination before there would be conversation. But their laughter continued. And, increasingly, as they rattled along, Amelia felt herself to be the butt of it. They had made a mock of the duchess. That, in its way had been bad enough. And then they had deliberately chosen her to abduct. And why? Because someone among them thought her so stuffy that she would benefit from it? Was that the answer? Was this Lord Darrow's way of letting her know his true opinion?

The carriage was turning into an alley now and from the alley into a courtyard. Then it came to a halt before a door lit by a torch set in the wall, and in the silence Amelia could hear the approaching sound of another carriage which, she imagined, must be carrying the other revelers to this destination.

The door was opened by a footman and, seeing that he wore the royal colors, Amelia realized that they were, indeed, at Carlton House, but clearly in a wing some distance from the grand, formal apartments of which she had heard so much. Indeed, the sitting room into which they were led, was cozy with a fire burning in the hearth and oak-paneled walls which gave a sense of warmth and intimacy.

"There now!" the gentleman declared, pulling off his mask. "Damme if we didn't do it up brown, and no mistake! Between the dancing and the laughing, I've all but winded myself. Never mind. A glass or two of Prinny's claret will put me right!"

"Mr. Hanger!" Amelia exclaimed. "Is it really you? And Lucy! How could you play such a prank?"

"As demure as a nun's hen, ain't she?" the

second lady declared. The cat's head had been removed to reveal a fair-haired damsel who looked like a porcelain doll. Her accent was of the *haut ton*, although the language certainly was not. "You can call me 'Billingsgate,'" she declared, throwing her mask into a corner with careless disregard.

This was one of the notorious Berrymores, Amelia realized, the young lady who was known for her ability to swear like a navvy. No doubt that was another reason Amelia had been chosen to abduct, it being figured that she would easily be shocked. Very well! The lady could say anything she liked! Amelia was determined that she would not turn a hair.

"Oh, it was such a lovely lark!" The Honorable Lucy Hanger declared, spinning about the room in order to collapse on the settee next to the fire. "Did you see the duchess's face?"

At that moment the door opened and a second part of the company arrived, consisting of three gentlemen, one of which, to Amelia's considerable surprise, was her brother.

"Randolph!" she exclaimed. "What are you doing here?"

"Dash it, he was determined not to let us get off with his sister without a struggle," a rough-and-ready-looking gentleman declared, rubbing his jaw where a black bruise was just beginning to appear.

"Are you all right, Amelia?" Randolph demanded, coming to put one arm about her.

"That's more than any one of us would do for a sister, eh, 'Newgate'?" Mr. Hanger cried.

Amelia turned curiously to look at the young Berrymore who had won his reputation by having been incarcerated from time to time in any number of English prisons for various imbroglios.

"Really, George," the Honorable Lucy Hanger replied. "I declare that I have never asked you to do anything for me."

"The trouble with George," the Berrymore called 'Newgate' declared, pouring himself a glass of claret from a decanter on a table in the corner, "is that he's as scaly a smudge as was ever born!"

This pleasantry was greeted with gales of laughter in which George himself joined, and the delicate "Billingsgate" could be heard declaring that "Newgate" was a needlewit and urging him to 'stubble it.'" All of which left Amelia more bemused than anything else, a condition which was not relieved when still another Berrymore called "Hellgate," whose scheme the escapade apparently had been, had climbed on a chair to announce a toast to the evening's festivities, in the midst of which another door at the other end of the room opened and Lord Darrow appeared in the company of the Prince of Wales himself.

"Hanger! 'Hellgate'!" the Prince declared. "Need I ask what you have been up to? My dear Lucy, have a care for the cushions of that settee. I believe the heel of your shoe has made a rent in one of them already. "My dear 'Newgate,' I am always delighted to see you making free with my wine. What have you and your sister been doing with those masks? But of course! I remember now! You meant to gate-crash someone's party. Hello! What have we here? Miss Didright. We met at Vauxhall. And Randolph, old chap. I was afraid that we had seen the last of you. Where have you been the past few days?"

Amelia looked past the Prince, who was wandering genially through the room, greeting each of his guests in turn, directly at Lord Darrow. She wanted to believe that he was startled to see her in such an unlikely place. She wanted to believe that he had known nothing of her abduction in advance implying, as that would, that he wished to make a mock of her. And yet she did not think she saw astonishment in his dark eyes.

The Honorable Lucy Hanger arose from the settee and went to take his arm. "You should have been with us, my dear Hugh!" she cried. "It was such fun! Only fancy! We had the duchess take the dance floor with us! And then we snatched ourselves a prize as we left. Of course Randolph *would* follow, not recognizing us. I understand he would have given 'Newgate' a beating if he had not pulled off his mask and identified himself."

Amelia looked away and bit her lip to keep it from trembling. What a fool she had been to think that she could be part of this Society! There was as much difference between her and the Honorable Lucy Hanger as there was between night and day. But this was the company in which Lord Darrow found himself at home! How he must scorn the stuffier levels of the *haut ton* where she, perforce, belonged. He had condescended to do her a service and in her heart she had taken it more seriously than she ever should have done. How absurd it must have seemed to him to have the duchess invite him to her soirée, and with what relief must he have left when it was done. Perhaps it was at his suggestion that the Berrymores and the Honorable Hangers had chosen to descend on the house in Portman Square. Perhaps he had even named her as someone who needed to be taken down a peg. Amelia knew that her imagination was carrying her away with it, but she, somehow, could not seem to exercise control.

Meanwhile, Lord Darrow had made no answer to the Honorable Lucy, although she was still hanging on his arm. Indeed, when he did break his silence, it was to address Amelia directly.

"I think all this does not meet with your approval, Miss Didright," he said.

Amelia did not know whether he was mocking her or not and, indeed, she did not care. Forgetting the Prince's presence, forgetting everything but her own sudden rage, she turned on the young marquess.

"What does it matter?" she demanded. "How can it possibly concern you, sir? Why, it is quite clear to me that your mind is so taken up with mighty matters that I would not like to offer you even the most casual distraction. And now, Randolph, I think that I would like to return home. But you will do me the favor of not accepting the use of a carriage if anyone offers it to you. I prefer a hackney cab. Good night, ladies. Gentlemen. Sir."

She paused before the Prince of Wales, confounded by her own boldness. "You must excuse my behavior if I seem to be abrupt," she said with a small curtsey. "But I am not accustomed to the ways of such an exclusive society, it seems."

She paused and turned back to look at Lord Darrow, knowing that she had said enough and yet, somehow, unable to stop. "I hope, sir," she said, "that you have been amused."

And then, because her brother was holding the door open for her and she could see the amazement in his eyes, Amelia turned and hurried out of the room. It was not until they were in a hackney cab, being driven up the Mall that she unclenched her hands and discovered that she had scratched the palms so badly with her nails that they were bleeding.

Chapter 17

"Of course her reputation is quite destroyed," the Duchess of Bradlaw said in her penetrating voice. "It was planned, of course. Everyone knows that. But the others were wise enough to disguise themselves. People can only speculate as to their identity. But when Amelia pretended to being abducted, she made a grave mistake. The tale is on everybody's tongue, I assure you, my dear Selina. I will be frank with you. They are calling her a jade."

Lady Didright sat huddled in her chair like a sparrow buffeting itself against the cold. And, indeed, there was a chill in the blue salon although a fire had been lit. Outside the rain streamed down the windows in a sullen way. It was eleven o'clock of the morning following the ball.

"I do not like to disagree, Dorelle," Lady Didright replied so meekly that she almost might not have spoken, "but when Amelia and her brother returned here last night, I had the distinct impression that it had been a most unpleasant experience for her which, had she been part of planning the prank, would not have been the case."

The duchess thrust out her nose, her chin and her bosom in an aggressive manner. "If you do not like to disagree with me, my dear Selina," she said, "then you should be careful not to do so. The fact of the matter no doubt, is that, the gel had realized her mistake. Or perhaps she was simply trying to deceive you. You must be prepared for that in future. Deceit. What did she tell you about the escapade? Did she admit that she and her brother were a part of it?"

Lady Didright gave the impression of being clad in drooping feathers rather than neat, gray taffeta. "She told me nothing beyond the fact that Randolph had come after her and brought her home and that—that she was quite safe. I was extraordinarily worried, you know, my dear Dorelle. And she and Randolph were thoughtful enough to send round a note to your house directly they arrived home."

The duchess sniffed. "Too kind of them, I'm sure. "But their thoughtfulness did not extend to telling you the truth."

"Amelia said that she was tired," Lady Didright replied. "And, indeed, she was as white as white can be. I asked after her this morning, but Elizabeth says that her bedchamber door is closed and bolted on the inside. I declare, I am quite worried about the poor child."

"She is not a poor child," the duchess said in a voice which seemed to march around the room. "She is a silly gel who has apparently made the most dangerous sort of social connections. All of which turned her head! Do not expect me to have patience with her, for I cannot manage it! To think that she and Randolph helped to plot such a disruption to my party! That makes it clear to you, I hope, that he intends to take money from you under false pretenses. Why, quite clearly he only pretends to give up his associations!"

Lady Didright rose from her chair and made an ineffectual attempt to dart about, but clearly she had not the heart for it.

"He claims that neither he nor Amelia knew anything about the debacle," she protested. "He said that he simply went after her and that it was not necessary, in the end, for him to have to persuade her captors to let her go. He said that it was all done in sport."

"Of course he would make excuses!" the duchess declaimed, puffing ever so slightly. "Sport, indeed! The party was quite ruined. You saw yourself how many of the company left, as soon as they decently could."

Lady Didright refrained from mentioning the fact that she had heard several departing guests declare that the contrast between a burst of spontaneous gaiety such as they had just seen and the actual ball itself had been such as to discourage them from remaining.

"It was a great pity, Dorelle," she murmured. "A great pity, indeed."

But the duchess shrugged off sympathy. Clearly it was a wrench to her to admit that any effort of hers had failed. "I suppose Randolph did not tell you who the masked dancers were," she said. "There were rumors last night, you know, that the Prince himself might have been among them."

"He—he did not give their names, it's true."

"Did you have the wit to ask him?"

"But of course I did, Dorelle. I knew you would like to know."

"Your son preferred to protect his friends?"

"I do not think that if they had been his friends they would have done that to Amelia. Believe me, Dorelle, she was truly shaken and I could tell that Randolph was much concerned."

"Much concerned that, now he had had his fun, you might put your foot down even more firmly than you did before, no doubt!" the duchess announced. "Truly you are such a ninny, Selina! You would believe anything anyone told you as long as they could manage to keep their face straight."

"He said that it was over and done with, and that the names did not matter!" Lady Didright said, showing some small defiance as she came to rest in the center of the room.

The duchess was a clever woman, and she knew that there were some areas on which she could not continue to press. Apparently Randolph's veracity was one of them.

"At least Lord Darrow cannot be accused of having been one of them," she said, taking another tack. "I admit that I was disappointed when he took such an abrupt leave. But I expect he had his reasons. And certainly, if he had known how we were shortly to be regaled, he would have been on hand to see it. That is, if he had had a hand in planning it."

A certain pained expression flitted across Lady Didright's eyes, giving the clear impression that she did not want to talk about Lord Darrow. Indeed, the duchess suspected that her friend found the entire conversation a dreadful strain, but she did not intend to let her off so easily. Selina was *weak*. That was the sum and substance of it. It was a wonder that she had got along on her own for so long. Now, of course, she could lose hold of the entire situation at any moment if she did not have advice.

"You know, of course, that you have only one choice when it comes to the matter of Amelia," the duchess said. "It is your good fortune that it is a course which will serve your future purposes well."

"Amelia!" Lady Didright exclaimed, as though her mind had flitted elsewhere, as, the duchess reflected, no doubt it had. "Oh, I do not think it is necessary to do anything about Amelia."

"But of course there is!" the duchess declared, removing herself from her chair with so much vigor that Lady Didright flew to press herself against a wall. "Amelia has clearly lost all sense of decorum. She has made one scandal of herself and she will soon make others unless you take appropriate steps! The gel must be sent to the country, and that without delay!"

"The country!" Lady Didright cried. "But that is quite impossible. I must remain in London with Elizabeth until the Season, and I would not like Amelia to be alone at Random Hall with no one but the servants to keep her company."

"On the contrary, Selina," the duchess said, pointing a long finger in her friend's direction in much the same manner that she would have aimed a gun, "that is precisely what the gel needs. A lot of solitude. An opportunity to regard the evil of her ways, to consider the embarassment she has been to you."

"But I did not consider it an embarassment!" Lady Didright exclaimed. "I was very anxious until she returned and I saw that she was quite safe, but . . ."

"An embarrassment!" the duchess continued in a voice which seemed to warn that she would brook no contradiction a second time. "In sending her back to Random Hall, you will be accomplishing two other aims as well. She will be kept out of Lord Darrow's way long enough to allow him an interest in Elizabeth, and you will be setting the pattern for the future when she will be your companion in the country."

"Oh dear!" Lady Didright wailed. "I am not at all certain that . . ."

"Quite right, my dear!" the duchess snapped. "You are not quite certain of anything, are you? Are you happy with the way things are going? Is this the best of all possible worlds?"

"No. Of course it is not," Lady Didright replied

hesitantly. "But I do not like to be so arbitrary with the poor child."

"You can put it to her this way," the duchess said. "Tell her that you are certain that her nerves will not stand the London pace. Pretend to be doing her a favor. Ah, I have the very bait! I should have thought of it before. Tell her that it is only in this way that she can avoid being snubbed by the very best people. That will frighten her as nothing else will do."

"My dear Dorelle," Lady Didright wailed. "You are so very arbitrary that sometimes you frighten me! I cannot think that it would be fair to Amelia . . ."

"When have you begun to think about what is *fair* to Amelia?" the duchess exclaimed. "When you asked me for help, you did not mention being fair. I would not have agreed to help you if you had."

Lady Didright unfurled her fan and made a great commotion with it. "Perhaps I should never have imposed my problems on you, Dorelle," she said. "Indeed, I am certain now that I should not. You have been too good, but . . ."

The duchess drew herself up to her full height, threatening to touch the ceiling with her turban-top. "Do not ask me to withdraw!" she cried. "I am not accustomed to having my efforts thwarted. I will not leave a job half done. My reputation would suffer for it. Why, I have dabbled in the affairs of half the people who were entertained at my house last night. Every one of them has watched our friendship ripen in recent days. They know I am helping you in family matters. Indeed, if you must know the truth, I have made no secret of it. That was why Amelia's so-called abduction was so upsetting to me. My friends will think that I do not have your problems firmly in hand. I intend to prove otherwise, my dear Selina! After all, I have my reputation to protect. I will continue as I have begun. With your father an invalid and Amelia in the country, we will turn our attention to your son, I think."

Lady Didright opened her mouth as though she were about to speak, but no sound was heard in the silent room except for the heaving of the duchess's breath. The exertion required to have made such an impassioned defense had taken its toll, and she stood gasping like a great, beached fish until a clearly frightened Lady Didright helped her to a chair.

"I cannot bear to be crossed in this!" the duchess wheezed.

"No, no. Of course you shall not be," her friend assured her, proceeding to dig behind the sofa pillows for a vinaigrette she remembered having tucked there. But when she tried to hold it beneath the duchess's nose, she was pushed away.

"Nonsense!" the duchess puffed. "I am quite myself again. It does not do me good to rail. Never mind. There is Randolph to deal with. Clearly, he did not take you seriously when you spoke to him about the money the other day. Last night his behavior was a public challenge, you understand. It had all been planned in advance with his connivance. He was to rush away to rescue his sister!

A public challenge to you, Selina! He must be taught a lesson! Indeed he must!"

"But really, my dear Dorelle, I think that you exaggerate," Lady Didright said hesitantly. "Much as I do not want you to lose your temper again, I really think I ought to say . . ."

"Have you given him the fifty guineas yet?" the duchess demanded.

"Well, actually, I intended to do that today," Lady Didright murmured. "I believe Randolph has arranged to meet Mr. Hanger at his club on purpose to pay him."

The duchess loosened the laces of her stomacher and leaned back in her chair. "Very well," she said. "You must refuse to give him the money when he applies for it. Tell him you are not convinced he means to keep his part of the bargain."

Lady Didright stared at her, clearly aghast. "But Mr. Hanger will expect to be paid!" she cried. "It would be dishonorable of Randolph to fail him."

"Do you not understand?" the duchess said wearily. "This is precisely what is wanted. If he cannot bring himself to throw the fast set off, then they must throw him off, instead. Even the Hangers and the Berrymores have a certain code. They may not pay their tailors from one year to the next, but they honor wagers between one another. If Randolph does not pay, he will no longer be a part of them. It is as simple as that."

Lady Didright fluttered from a chair to the settee and back to the chair again. "Oh, dear!" she wailed. "I do not like to think of a son of mine in that sort of debt. Randolph will be stricken if I do anything of the sort. It makes it worse for him, you see, because the estate will all be his in another year. And yet I know he is too proud to explain the state of things to Mr. Hanger. It is a humiliation to a young man to be handed out money by his mother, particularly if she puts terms to it. I see that now."

The duchess leaned forward with an effort. "Do you want him to be a part of that handful of rogues?" she said ominously. "Do you want your own son to ruin himself?"

"Of course not, dear Dorelle!" Lady Didright exclaimed. "But if I do not let him use his judgment . . ."

She was interrupted by a rap on the door, followed by the appearance of a footman who announced that Lord Darrow was calling and wished to see Miss Amelia Didright.

The duchess threw her friend a glance pregnant with meaning. "You see?" she muttered. "It is imperative that she be sent off to the country. For the present it should be sufficient to have the message confused. Make certain that word is sent up for Miss Elizabeth to come down at once."

Oh dear! Oh dear!" Lady Didright wailed. "I wish I was quite certain what was the right thing to do."

The duchess gathered herself together and sat up very straight. "There is no need for you to think of right and wrong, my dear," she said.

"Right and wrong are beside the point, which is something you have never really understood. Follow my suggestions. That is absolutely all that is necessary. And let Lord Darrow be sent in at once."

Chapter 18

Upstairs in her bed-chamber, Amelia sat on the window seat, and looked out over the rooftops of that part of the city which thrust its way north from Portman Square. Could it be, she wondered, that she had ever even half expected that somewhere in this vast metropolis she would find happiness? London had meant glamor and excitement and the lurking chance that at any moment she might turn about and meet the eyes of the gentleman she was destined to find. Girlish hopes, perhaps. Hopes which she had kept well hidden under a sensible exterior. But even when she had been little more than her mother's companion there had been excitement in the air, the sense that the sort of happiness she had never known might be right around the corner.

And for awhile, when it seemed to be coming

true, she had not quite been able to believe it. Always in the back of her mind there was the fear that something would occur to keep her from her newly declared independence. And, as for Lord Darrow, she had not dared to allow herself to even daydream. Now it would seem that she had done well to be so cautious.

She had *not* been hurt, she told herself, clenching her hands in the lap of her white muslin morning gown. Humiliated, in a sense, she had been, for she thought she had been mocked. If only Mr. Hanger and the Berrymores had been involved she could have borne it very well indeed. But Lord Darrow had been part of the plan. She still remembered the way the Honorable Lucy Hanger had clung on his arm. How intimately she had talked to him. Ladies such as she and Miss Berrymore were fun-loving sophisticates of the sort Lord Darrow had doubtless been surrounded by all his life. He was comfortable with them. They were his equals in that exclusive circle ranged about the Prince. And she, Amelia, was an outsider. She could never have been made to feel it more acutely than she had the night before at Carlton House. Lord Darrow had arranged it. And it had been cruel of him. Cruel!

But then his friends did not know the difference between a joke and an embarrassment. Mama had been right in one thing. They were not the sort of people Randolph should have traffic with. He should pay his debt to Mr. Hanger and have done. No doubt he saw that now himself. He had been very quiet during their return the night before, and there had been a brooding look in his eyes which Amelia had never seen there before.

As for herself, well, she had learned a lesson. She was indeed as sensible as her mother had always claimed her to be. London was no place for her. In time the frivolity of the *haut ton* would have become intolerable. Someone like Elizabeth would do very well indeed in this Society. Elizabeth and Lord Darrow—two of a kind if they but knew it. Selfish. Heartless. Enjoying themselves at the expense of others. What a perfect prig he must have thought her for refusing to discuss Randolph's problem in obtaining funds. No wonder he had been pleased enough to see her made the butt of his friends' little joke! Having worked herself into something of a fury, Amelia jumped up from the window seat and called impatiently for Doris.

The abigail had been waiting just outside the chamber door for the better part of the morning for just such an opportunity to see her favorite mistress. Elizabeth had told her what had happened at the duchess's ball and, as always, had colored the account with her own conclusions.

"First they made a fool of the duchess and then one of my sister," she had declared triumphantly. "Of course, Randolph went rushing after them but it was over an hour before we heard that they were safe at home. Mama flew into the boughs, of course. But do you think that either one of them would tell her where they had been? I declare, I quite lost my patience with them both and Mama should have done the same. But she would say that she was only relieved that they had not come to any harm. Such a stupid evening in so many ways! I cannot think why Lord Darrow should have left quite so precipitately, but then I expect he will tell me when we next meet."

Now Doris took one look at Amelia and breathed a deep sigh of relief. "I was afraid that I might find you distraut," she said. "Miss Elizabeth told me all about it, or as much as she knows."

"Which is very little," Amelia said more sharply than was her custom. "I do not want to think of it, Doris. It was an unpleasant experience and I intend to forget it as soon as possible. Tell me. Who is with my grandfather?"

"The doctor came quite early this morning, miss," the abilgail replied, "and prescribed I don't know how many medicines, all of which Lord Wellingham said he would not take. When the doctor said he intended to send another woman to nurse him, his Lordship said that if he did, he would not answer for what might happen. But then the doctor muttered things to him—I could not hear what he was saying—and your grandfather turned quite white, miss, and took his teeth out of his mouth and let himself be fed a quantity of laudanum. Nelly, the kitchenmaid is sitting with him. There's naught to do except to watch him sleep."

Amelia pressed the knuckles of her clenched hands together. "If I needed any other argument to convince me of what to do, what you have just said is quite sufficient," she declared. "Pack my portmanteaux, Doris! I intend to take my grandfather into the country and Randolph, too, if I can convince him."

And leaving the startled abigail staring after her, Amelia hurried out of the room, only to encounter her sister passing through their little sitting room. Elizabeth was dressed in an exquisite morning costume of lilac gauze and satin with her golden curls framing her lacey mobcap.

"My dear Amelia!" she exclaimed. "Where are you going is such a rush? Why, I declare, Mama will not be pleased to see you downstairs. You are to rest, she says, since your nerves must have been sorely tried last night. Poor dear. You must have been terribly humiliated. You should have seen yourself being dragged out of the room like that. And Randolph rushing after you, as though he really thought that you might come to harm. You have become notorious in a matter of minutes. Such a pity, really. You would have done better never to have fancied yourself a *femme fatale*."

"What makes you so spiteful, Elizabeth?" Amelia demanded, barring the door by standing in front of it. "I have put up with this behavior from you for far too long."

"You mean to go back to your old ways, then?" her sister replied. "Nipping and nagging at any opportunity."

Amelia longed to shake her and refrained only by making a considerable effort. "I am not rebuking you," she said. "If I comment on your character, as I intend to do, that is quite a different thing. You are spoiled and selfish and not at all as beautiful as you pretend to be. Far from having made a great splash in London Society, you have caused very few ripples indeed. You behave like a silly wench when you are in company and like a pampered brat the rest. If anyone is to be pitied it is you. You must be truly unhappy or you would not treat others the way you do. At least that is the only excuse I can think of! No doubt I am being far too kind."

Elizabeth had opened her mouth to reply less than halfway through this speech, but when she had the opportunity to get in a word, it was apparent that none could be found. Slowly her face drained of color and she stared at Amelia with a strange expression in her eyes. Clearly, facing the truth about herself had been a frightful shock.

And then a rap sounded on the door and Amelia answered it to find the footman waiting in the hall with the message that Lady Didright required Miss Elizabeth to come to the blue salon as soon as possible in order to receive a caller, Lord Darrow.

Elizabeth's response was to give a little cry and hurry out of the room and down the stairs while Amelia, closing the door behind her, felt quite numb. Was he willing to go this far to taunt her, then? And for what reason except that she might have appeared too cold, too given to restraint. But that was absurd, of course! He was not punishing her. She mattered too little in his scheme of things for him to trouble himself. He was amusing himself. Nothing more. No doubt the day before he had mentioned to his cronies that he was to attend a tiresome soirée in order to do a favor for an awkward country girl. Perhaps even the idea of the masked interruption had been his idea.

"It will give some life to the affair, at any rate," he may have told them.

And today? Well, today he meant to amuse himself in another way. He could not have failed to notice that Elizabeth was infatuated with him. Certainly she had taken every pain to show it. And perhaps he thought that she was intrigued as well, although, as Amelia told herself, she had given him no reason to. And now he was entertaining himself by hoping to play them off against one another. That he would do such a thing was the final disillusionment. The sooner she could put London behind her, the better!

Sending Doris to the kitchen for a tray to be brought to her grandfather, Amelia went down the hall, encountering Randolph just outside the door to the old man's bedchamber. Motioning him to accompany her inside, Amelia dismissed the kitchenmaid and pulled the curtains wide to let the spring sunlight in. The canopied bed seemed to dwarf Lord Wellingham who lay quite still, his sunken cheeks and general pallor being quite sufficient to cause a general alarm.

"It may be possible that Dr. Pinchpurse is right," Randolph murmured. But Amelia protested that could not be the case.

"How else is Grandpapa to look when he has

been kept for the main on gruel and deprived of his teeth?" she demanded. "Furthermore, the doctor has told him such tales about disease in general and the state of his own health in particular as to sap him of his resistance. I have lost all patience with Mama. It is my guess that the duchess is behind everything that has happened, but Mama must take the blame for having given in to her. I propose that you and I and Grandpapa return to Random Hall directly, before our lives are scrambled any further."

And, leaving Randolph to consider that option, Amelia went over to the bed and kissed and coaxed the old man until his eyes finally opened. Briskly, she plumped his pillows and helped him to sit up against them, which effort gave his sagging cheeks some color. Next the ivory teeth were inserted gently. This having been accomplished, Lord Wellingham cast a wild glance or two about the room and declared that Dr. Pinchpurse would be no end annoyed if he were to return and find his patient even partly vertical.

"Damme, gel," the old man said weakly, "there must be something in what he says, I feel so poorly."

"And so would I if I had been dosed with laudanum as you have," Amelia retorted. "To say nothing of having been kept too much on gruel. See. Here is Doris with a tray. Just put it there. Randolph, help her clear a space. Throw those bottles away. And the paper packets as well. Doris. Keep guard outside the door. I do not care what you have to say, but keep us from being interrupted."

There was chicken on the tray the abigail had brought and some oyster patties, together with a bit of bread and cheese, not to mention a pewter mug brimming full with ale. Lord Wellingham's old eyes began to sparkle the moment he saw it and a few sips were sufficient for him to declare that he felt quite recovered.

"I do not know the way of it, my dear," he said, "but when you are with me and I've a bit of proper food and drink under my belt I feel that I could pop out of this bed quite nimble-like. But then Pinchpurse appears, and I'm somehow at death's door again. I feel it here and here and here."

Pointing to the general direction of his heart, his liver and his stomach with one hand, he picked at the chicken breast with the other. "But just now," he continued, "I feel as right as rain, as Queensberry likes to say."

"His Lordship sent a messenger asking after you, Grandpapa," Randolph said. "Yesterday morning and again today. I was to tell you, but every time I looked in you were sleeping."

"Damme, Old Q would never have let this happen to him," Lord Wellingham declared, wiping the foam of the ale off his upper lip with the back of his arm in an indelicate way which was so much like his normal custom that Amelia was greatly cheered. "He always said the only doctor a man should pay is the doctor who stands to benefit from keeping him alive."

"Listen to me, Grandpapa," Amelia murmured, kneeling beside the bed. "Things have gone wrong for you, and they have gone wrong for Randolph and me, as well. There is no time to go into the particulars. You know about Randolph being kept without funds unless he agrees to certain terms. And there are other factors which make London odious to me. I want you to accompany me back to Random Hall. Far away from the duchess and Dr. Pinchpurse and . . . and certain other people who shall be nameless."

She was interrupted by an outcry outside the door. "I am sorry, sir!" she heard Doris cry. "You cannot enter this room!"

But apparently the abigail was pushed aside, for the door flew open and Dr. Pinchpurse himself appeared, accompanied by a sluttish-looking woman of the same variety as Mrs. Bundy. Pushing his tray aside, Lord Wellingham cowered against the pillows. Randolph raised his fists in an aggressive fashion. And Amelia leaped to her feet.

"Perhaps someone would like to explain to me precisely what is going on?" the doctor announced, propelling himself across the room with the swinging of his long arms and a sidelong fling of his sharp nose. "Lady Didright will be informed that my directions have been disobeyed. And the duchess, as well. I declare young lady, how is it that you are so determined to kill your own grandfather? Because that is what you are doing, I assure you. If he has consumed more than half that cup of ale, he may have a stroke directly. In fact I believe that I see certain signs . . ."

"Randolph!" Amelia cried. "Strike him if he takes one step closer to that bed! Doris! Make certain that this—this creature is not allowed to lay a hand on Grandpapa. I am going downstairs to have this out with Mama once and for all!"

Chapter 19

There was an oval mirror framed in gilt hanging on the landing of the stairs and Amelia paused there for a brief moment to put to rights her disheveled curls and straighten the gauze tucker which filled the low-necked bodice of her sprigged, blue muslin gown. More than anything she wanted to present a calm exterior, although fury threatened to engulf her. She could not plan the words that she meant to say. She could not really even think in a coherent way. All that she knew was that she was not content to stand aside for a moment longer.

The footman glanced at her curiously as she passed and Amelia knew that he would have hurried to open the doors of the blue salon for her if he had guessed her direction. But before he could make a move, she had turned the knob and was advancing into the room.

Once there, she was forced to pause to take her bearings. The duchess sat in the Chippendale wing chair, nodding her turban over a cup of tea. On the striped silk settee opposite, Amelia's mother perched in her bird-like manner, half turned to stare anxiously at her elder daughter. Lord Darrow was standing beside the mantelpiece, his handsome face a mask of dark reserve. The sight of him gave Amelia pause, for in her fury she had forgotten that he was here. And then she remembered that he had called on Elizabeth. The thought was as painful now as it had been when she had first heard it. Her sister sat close beside where the marquess was standing, her golden-haired beauty glowing in the shadow on a Chinese screen, and as though to prove a point of her own, she chose this moment to smile up at him in much the same fashion that the Honorable Lucy Hanger had smiled the night before. And that was quite sufficient to strengthen Amelia's resolution.

"My dear child!" her mother exclaimed. "Such a clatter! That is no way to enter a room, surely!"

"She only does it to annoy, Mama," Elizabeth declared. "She does it to make a point of interrupting us!"

"If she were my daughter," the duchess said, "I would have her leave the room and enter again, only this time with more decorum."

"My dear duchess," Amelia said in a clear and carrying voice, "I am *not* your daughter, this is *not* your house and my grandfather is *not* your responsibility. I mean to ask you to keep that in mind. Not that it will be any concern of mine what you do or say after today, since neither I nor my grandfather will be in this house and subject to the fruits of your suggestions."

Amelia was determined not to look at Lord Darrow but she sensed that he was listening to her carefully. No doubt she was making herself ridiculous, but she did not care. This was not the sort of moment which could be put off. What must be said, must be said now.

"Have you gone quite mad, my dear?" Lady Didright demanded, darting to her feet. "You cannot say such things to one of my dearest friends!"

"It seems that I have done so, Mama!" Amelia declared. "And there is more, a great deal more!"

"Make her stop, Mama!" Elizabeth cried. "Why, she is on a rampage. You should have heard the things she said to me upstairs. I meant to tell you later. *That* was unpleasant enough, I assure you. I never dreamed that she would bring her wild attacks into the salon."

"I will take them into the streets if necessary," Amelia assured her. "This is no joke, Elizabeth. Serious matters are at issue here, including an old man's life."

The duchess who had slowly set her teacup in its saucer on the table before her, was sitting very stiff and straight. The only sign she gave of being perturbed was that her bosom heaved so violently that the ivory brooch she wore on the bodice of her gown was thrown about like a floundering ship on a restless sea.

"So this is the way my efforts on your behalf are to be rewarded, Selina?" she said in a menacing voice. "I might have known that you would not be willing to make sufficient effort. At least you must understand now why, in my opinion, this gel should be safely hidden away in the country. Apparently *she* has the wit to see that, as well. London is no place for chits who do not know the meaning of truly polished behavior."

"If by polished behavior you mean a combination of hypocrisy and deceit, then I am glad enough to be as I am," Amelia told her. Now that her anger had been unbound, she found that she was taken with fits of shivering which she could only hide by wrapping her arms around one another. "No doubt Randolph would have demonstrated polished behavior if he had refused to honor his debt to Mr. Hanger under the terms my mother— at your suggestion I believe—laid down, terms calculated to humiliate him by keeping him away from his friends."

"I may have given my advice," the duchess snapped. "I often do when it is asked for. This is the first time I have been condemned for doing so, I assure you! Generally my friends have the good grace to offer thanks for having been told what they should do for their own good."

"It *was* for Randolph's own good not to associate with that dreadful group, dear," Lady Didright said in a timid voice.

"You mean the group Lord Darrow is a member of?" Amelia said. "The Prince's circle?"

"Oh dear!" Lady Didright exclaimed. "I quite forgot!"

"Amelia led you to say it!" Elizabeth cried. "She will create havoc where she can."

"I think it strange," Amelia said, "that even though he is a friend to Hanger and the others, Lord Darrow was invited to attend an entertainment at your house, your Grace. I was here when you issued it, and as I recall you pressed him warmly to be there. And yet you have admitted to advising my mother to blackmail my brother, in a sense, to keep him away from the very company Lord Darrow enjoys. I must confess I find that very strange. One would almost think that it was somehow politic to make an exception of Lord Darrow. And, pray, why would that be?"

Lady Didright was clearly in a state of such distraction that she could no longer weigh her words. "He is so right for Elizabeth, Amelia!" she cried and then, directly having said the words, she pressed her fingers to her lips. "Oh dear!" she murmured. "I only meant that since she seems to be so attracted to rogues and it is necessary for her to keep out of trouble by being married . . ."

"Selina!" the duchess exclaimed, lifting herself to her feet in order to glower more directly down at her friend. "Say no more, I implore you! Say no more!"

"Yes. All of this is beside the real point," Amelia said quickly, aware of the intensity with which Lord Darrow was watching her and equally conscious that a faux pas of magnificent proportion had been made. As if to reinforce this point, Elizabeth fled the room, her face buried in her hands.

"My primary concern is for my grandfather," Amelia continued. "I had hoped that Lord Darrow might have something convincing enough to tell you about Dr. Pinchpurse to discourage you from allowing him to attend Grandpapa."

"You knew he meant to speak to me on the subject?" Lady Didright demanded curiously.

"Indeed, I asked him specifically to do so," Amelia replied.

"You asked him to give his opinion of my personal physician?" the duchess demanded, bridling. "*My* word was not good enough for you?"

Amelia did not lower her eyes. Indeed, she continued to face the duchess defiantly. "I myself saw nothing to recommend the gentleman in question," she replied. "It was because of you, madam, that my grandfather was made to fear for his health in the first place and your doctor subsequently took every opportunity to reinforce what you had said. My grandfather is an old man and, since he is not a fool, he is aware of his own mortality. Horror stories about men of his age and younger who had succumbed in every manner of ghastly ways are bound to make an old man fearful. Cause him to imagine symptoms. Then he is deprived of his teeth and fed gruel which is bound to weaken him. Then given laudanum to confuse his faculties. It does not take much of such treatment to administer a *coup de grâce*. Tell me, your Grace, is that what was intended?"

"Amelia!" Lady Didright cried. "You must not

say such things. I only meant to keep him to the house, out of Queensberry's way. And then when Dr. Pinchpurse said that he was actually ill, why I believed him. And then . . ."

But she was interrupted by the duchess who was marching to the door, delivering herself of a philippic as she went. Never, she declared, had she been so insulted! To be called a murderess to her face! This was a fine way for her unselfish devotion to a friend to be rewarded! She would go straight to her solicitor! Lay claim to having been libelled in the worst degree! She would teach Amelia to watch her tongue in future! Indeed, she would have a terrible revenge!

As soon as the door closed behind her, Lady Didright broke into a flood of tears. As for Lord Darrow, he seemed torn between speech and silence and apparently decided on the latter, looking very grim.

"I meant to take Lord Darrow's advice and relieve Dr. Pinchpurse of his duties," Lady Didright wailed. "Indeed, I should have done so directly had it not been that the house has been in so much turmoil all the morning with the duchess advising me what steps to take now that you have lost your reputation, my dear! I only meant to do what was best."

At that Lord Darrow stepped forward. "Your daughter has not lost her reputation, Lady Didright," he said in a low voice. "She was the victim of a practical joke which, had I known of it in advance, I would never have allowed to occur."

"You did not know?" Amelia murmured.

"Do you believe I would have countenanced anything of the sort, Miss Didright? Or the Prince either, for that matter? Both of us gave Hanger and the others something to think about after you and your brother left Carlton House last night."

"Carlton House!" Lady Didright exclaimed. "You were taken there, Amelia? Oh dear, what can all this mean?"

"It means that some of my acquaintances have been inordinately foolish, madam," Lord Darrow replied. "I can only say that they meant no harm. That was what I came to tell your daughter."

"You came to see Elizabeth, sir, not me."

"That was the duchess's decision," Lady Didright gasped. "She had the message sent up to Elizabeth instead of you. It was part of her grand scheme . . ."

"To wed your younger daughter to a rogue, madam?" Lord Darrow said in a low voice. "Did she really believe that she could manipulate me?"

"In my opinion, it is the duchess's firm belief that she can manipulate anyone," Amelia declared. "Well, she knows better now, at any rate."

"I believe she must, Miss Didright," the young marquess said with the hint of a smile. "You put your position to her very clearly, if you will permit me to say it."

"Dear Amelia has always been so sensible," Lady Didright declared. "I wonder I could ever have thought otherwise."

"Mama, you are quite incorrigible!" Amelia cried. It was very strange, indeed, but she felt like bursting into laughter. She realized that it had been a very long time since her heart had felt so light.

"As to that, I cannot say," Lady Didright replied. "I only know that Randolph shall have his fifty guineas with no strings attached. And as for Dr. Pinchpurse . . ."

"He is upstairs this very moment," Amelia told her. "At least he was when I left Grandpapa's bedchamber. Randolph is holding him at bay."

Lady Didright raised her chin in a determined fashion. "Then I will see that the gentleman is dismissed," she declared. "And if there is trouble, perhaps you will be willing to be of further assistance, Lord Darrow."

"It will be my pleasure, madam," the young marquess replied. "I have enough evidence against him to send him speeding out of the country, I believe."

"Dear Lord Darrow," Lady Didright murmured, presenting him with her hand. "You will not mind if I leave you alone with Amelia for a moment while I see to my responsibilities?"

"You could not have presented me with a more pleasant option," he replied. And then, as soon as she had darted from the room, he turned his full attention to Amelia. For a long moment neither of them spoke.

"I—I would like to thank you for everything you have done, sir," Amelia said at last.

His eyes traced the curve of her cheek and lingered on her lips. "I will be well rewarded," he said in a low voice, "if you will tell me that you no longer plan to leave London. Is it too much to hope that you will change your mind?"

"I believe my mother would tell you that I am far too sensible than to do otherwise," she murmured with a smile. "Yes, I begin to think that it would suit me very well to stay."

"And I will see that in staying you have no regrets," he told her.

"I believe you will do precisely what you say, sir," Amelia said slowly, moving into the shelter of his arms. "And, since it seems I am so sensible, I do not think anything will prove me wrong."

Chapter 20

A thousand candles blazed in the four great crystal chandeliers which graced the ballroom at Carlton House. At the head of the great staircase, the Prince of Wales, magnificently dressed, stood welcoming his guests. Only a few members of the dazzling assembly, however, were granted entry to the anteroom where the King and Queen sat on a dais.

"Why, Her Majesty is more comely than I had thought her," Amelia declared as the footmen on either side of the narrow door waved them forward toward the Royal couple who were surrounded by their intimates. "And he does not look as though he had been ill."

"The attacks come and go," Lord Darrow told her, pressing her arm close to his side. "The Prince took advantage of his father being in good health

216

at present to honor his parents with this ball. They are a quiet couple, you know, and would be as willing as not to remain quietly at Windsor. But, of course, the Prince is right. They should be seen. And his sisters are starved for excitement, as you have already seen."

Amelia smiled. On their way down the length of the ballroom, they had seen the Royal Princesses waiting with their partners for the first quadrille. They were not at all attractive ladies, with their heavy Hanoverian features, and it was feared it might be difficult to find husbands for them but for tonight, at least, they seemed determined to be happy.

Indeed, it was beyond Amelia's belief that anyone in the world could be sad. Never before had life seemed so fascinating to her. How was it, she often wondered, that she had never before had a full appreciation for the brilliance of a starlight night or the perfect perfume of a rose. Love had brought loveliness in its wake and she seemed to see the world untarnished, as she had done when she had been a child. Even the Royal couple before her seemed, somehow, more splendid than the rather ordinary people it was rumored that they were. Life was a fairy tale come true.

The formalities of being presented to Royalty were soon accomplished. Watching Hugh chatting to the King, Amelia found herself admiring the easy self-assurance of his ways. How many years would have to pass, she wondered, before she found nothing about that chiseled profile to admire? Surely the day would never come when his glance would not set her blood racing, as it did now when he turned to her. Because he had told her that he liked simplicity best, Amelia had chosen a demure, white *circassienne* gown which fastened tightly down the front with silver hooks and eyes. The look he cast her left no doubt in Amelia's mind that he found her charming.

In order to leave the Royal presence, it was necessary to back out the door, gentlemen making a bow and ladies a curtsy. As Amelia and Lord Darrow were preparing to take their departure in the customary way, the Prince of Wales appeared on the scene and bowed before the Queen, his mother.

"You will do me the honor of the first quadrille, madam," he said. "I am told there is a new tune to be played and that it bears your title, if not your name—*The Queen's Quadrille*. It has a certain ring to it, I think."

"It is a great thing to see them reconciled for the moment," Lord Darrow said in a low voice as they succeeded in leaving the anteroom and the Prince had passed them, smiling, with Queen Charlotte on his arm. "She does not often approve of anything he either says or does, which further drives him to rebellion, I sometimes think. But for tonight, at least, they seem content with one another."

"All the world must be content," Amelia replied, "if for no better reason than that I would have it so."

"What better reason could there be for anything?" he answered her in a teasing voice. "Come! The music is striking up. We must take the floor."

Amelia looked up at him. How dark his face seemed in contrast to his yellow, satin coat and the layered white of his cravat.

"Would you think it foolish of me if we did not move?" she asked him. "I would like to set this moment in my mind precisely so that when, in future, I am asked when I was truly happy, I can recall every detail of the here and now."

"On the contrary," he told her, "I would think you very wise indeed. So wise, in fact, that I shall go about impressing the moment on myself in the same manner."

And so they stood together beside one of the columns wrapped with coils of flowers which decorated the ballroom, their clasped hands hidden by the folds of Amelia's gown.

The violins struck up a pretty tune and the couples on the floor took their places in groups of four. The Prince and his mother were joined by the Duchess of Devonshire who was sporting a towering wig and whose partner might or might not be the duke, for all Amelia knew or cared. How well it suited her tonight to be alone with Hugh in the midst of the festivities. How well it suited her to watch and savor her own happiness.

"I knew Grandpapa would enjoy himself," she said and nodded in the direction of the platform where the musicians were playing. There, centrally situated between violins and the pianoforte, Lord Wellingham sat with Lord Queensberry, glass eye and all, beside him.

"They said they must be in a spot where they could see the ladies to best advantage," Amelia continued with a smile, "and the Prince was good enough to see that they were obliged. Mama will be beside herself."

"With Lord Berrymore to distract her, I doubt that she will have the time to notice," Hugh replied. "I asked him to pay her special attention and he is rogue enough to know precisely how."

And, sure enough, Amelia saw her mother busy on the dance floor, executing a complicated figure of the dance with "Hellgate" at her side.

"Oh dear!" Amelia cried, pressing her fingers to her lips. "Do you think she knows the company she is in?"

"Just at the moment, I do not think she cares," Lord Darrow replied. "That scowl would seem to indicate concentration on the steps and nothing more."

And, indeed, the care that Lady Didright was taking in darting to and fro was a marvel to perceive while, further down the line, Lord Berkeley whirled the Honorable Lucy Hanger about to her obvious delight. As for Randolph, handsome in a scarlet coat, his partner was the lady familiarly called "Billingsgate" whom he had somehow set to laughing so hard that she could scarcely dance.

"Damme, sir!" Amelia heard her cry as they swept by, "you keep me in the whoops. I'll be a nodd's cock if you don't!"

The music rose and the colors of the dancers' costumes seemed to make a kaleidoscope of the shifting scene. Elizabeth, an angel in pink satin and billowing lace, floated across the floor, holding her hand high for the Honorable George Hanger to clasp and flashing her sister and Lord Darrow a smile, as though to assure them that she was quite reconciled to the situation as, indeed, Amelia thought she was.

Faster and faster the music spun. Faster and faster the dancers twirled. The sound of giddy laughter rose in counterpoint to the melody.

"What are we doing standing here?" Lord Darrow said with a fond smile. "We should be in the midst of them, dancing the night away."

Their eyes met and suddenly they seemed to be standing in a pool of silence.

"How strange that I cannot hear the music," Amelia whispered.

And, indeed, they might as well have been alone together as in a crowd. And, with their eyes still locked together, they were seen to stray toward the balcony outside. An arm steals around a slender waist. And, as *The Queen's Quadrille* came to an end, the shadows claimed them.

ROMANCE From Fawcett Books

Let COVENTRY Give You
A Little Old-Fashioned Romance

☐ **RENEGADE GIRL** 50198 $1.50
by Mary Ann Gibbs

☐ **LORD BRANDSLEY'S BRIDE** 50020 $1.50
by Claire Lorel

☐ **DANCE FOR A LADY** 50201 $1.50
by Eileen Jackson

☐ **KIT AND KITTY** 50202 $1.50
by Sarah Carlisle

☐ **THE SMITHFIELD BARGAIN** 50203 $1.50
by Rachelle Edwards

☐ **CAROLINA** 50205 $1.50
by Leonora Blythe

GREAT ADVENTURES IN READING

☐ CAITLYN McGREGOR   14413 $2.95
  by Kitt Brown
  *The story of a woman of the American frontier with a dream to
  build a homestead in the wilds of Kentucky.*

☐ HELLBORN   14414 $2.50
  by Gary Brandner
  *A novel of demonic terror and possession. A terrifying demon
  chooses his bride and a horrifying method to possess her.*

☐ FORBIDDEN WINE   14419 $2.95
  by Fiona Harrowe
  *Set in the fourteenth century, this is the tale of a woman trapped by
  passion and bound by a love she could never have.*

☐ LOVER'S CHOICE   14420 $2.25
  by Cynthia Blair
  *A tale for young adults about two beautiful but very different sis-
  ters who learn to accept themselves as women and like each other
  as friends.*

☐ THE UNINVITED GUEST   14421 $2.50
  by Barbara Kennedy
  *The perfection of Dan Griswold's Florida citrus empire is marred
  when a dead body floats ashore during his granddaughter's wed-
  ding reception.*

Buy them at your local bookstore or use this handy coupon for ordering.